MMC

LAR

BULLET BARRICADE

BULLET BARRICADE

Leslie Ernenwein

CHIVERS

British Library Cataloguing in Publication Data available

This Large Print edition published by AudioGO Ltd, Bath, 2013.
Published by arrangement with Golden West Literary Agency

U.K.   Hardcover   ISBN   978 1 4713 1700 2
U.K.   Softcover   ISBN   978 1 4713 1701 9

Printed and bound in Great Britain by
MPG Books Group Limited

BULLET BARRICADE

BULLET BARRICADE

CHAPTER ONE

This was Sonora, with moon's shadowless sun scorching the high-walled slot of the Barranca Prieta, where one man crouched behind a scabrous rock reef while another man lay groaning on the ground. Beyond them, protected by a protruding ledge, stood a sorrel horse whose heaving sides dripped sweat; farther up the canyon a dust-veiled herd of cattle tromped steadily north-ward in desperate retreat.

The man on the ground propped himself on an elbow. He gagged and spat blood and said, "I got something to tell you, Clay — something important."

Clay Spain fired two shots before turning away from the reef. Dirty and dog-tired, he moved with a slow-motion reluctance, keeping his tall frame hunched so that it wouldn't be skylined. His blue eyes were bloodshot from lack of sleep, but there was a devil-be-damned glint in them as he said,

"We'll make another run for it, Dan, soon as the pony gets his wind back."

"Run, hell," Dan Tennant scoffed. He glanced at the bloody makeshift bandage across his chest: "You expect a man to keep going with a slug in his lung?" Blood got into Tennant's throat and choked him. He mumbled a curse in the confused, slobbering way of a drunken man; he wheezed, "Give my share to Lace Fayette at Hondo."

Spain peered at him, marveling that this pain-prodded man should be thinking about a girl. "You sure she's in Hondo?" he asked.

Tennant nodded.

"Don't recall her being there."

"She must've come after you left," Tennant said. He picked up a canteen and waggled it. "Not much water."

"Take what you want," Spain said. "I'll drink at Cartridge Creek this evening."

He went to the reef, picked up the Winchester, and fired a single shot. "Just so they'll know I'm still awake," he said, and came back to where Tennant lay.

"Don't let them others talk you out of it," Tennant warned. "I want Lace to have my share."

A cynical smile altered Spain's high-boned cheeks. He used his dangling shirttail to wipe his wet hands, then took out his

Durham sack and rolled a cigarette. "So she's the reason you wanted to get rich in Mexico," he mused.

"Have I got your promise?" Tennant demanded.

"Sure," Spain said, and dodged instinctively as a ricocheting bullet whanged past his head. "A queer time to be thinking about a girl," he said.

"Girl, hell," Tennant said. "Lace Fayette is a woman!" Some secret thought brightened his eyes; for this brief interval he seemed oblivious of pain and his voice was mild with remembering when he said, "The only woman I ever wanted so bad I could taste it."

That seemed odd to Spain. He had known Dan Tennant for upwards of two years; had worked and slept and eaten with him; had ridden the ciénaga bogs and patronized El Tanque's cantinas with him. Yet in all that time Dan had never mentioned Lace Fayette.

"Must be quite a woman," Spain reflected.

Tennant smiled as if savoring some past pleasure. "Most of the men in Apache Basin had a case on her. Even Lew Wade."

Thinking back to the time he had worked on Wade's ranch, Spain said, "I thought Lew was womanproof. All he seemed to care about was keeping Boxed W the big spread."

Ignoring that, Tennant asked, "You'll make sure Lace gets my share, won't you, Clay?"

Spain nodded.

"She staked me," Tennant said. "It was her money I put into your pooler outfit."

Blood got into his throat again. He gasped for breath with his mouth wide open. He rolled over on his belly and spewed red vomit into the dust. "Those *bandido* bastards," he whimpered.

And then he died.

Clay Spain looked at Tennant, remembering that Dan had been his first partner in the pooler outfit, the bold enterprise whereby six renegade Americans had built the beginnings of a cattle empire in Mexico. Easy money, they'd thought; big money. Arranging a percentage deal with dollar-grabbing *politicos,* they had stamped their Roman Six brand on a thousand calves the first year. The pooler outfit had seemed destined for fabulous success until Emiliano Zapata's rebel hordes drove the *federalistas* from power in Sonora. After that it was a case of run or die for gringo cowmen.

Spain glanced at Tennant's slack-jawed graying face again; he said, "Easy money, hell."

10

Then he picked up the canteen and went back to the rock reef.

The raiders were advancing cautiously, using boulders and protruding ledges for cover; they were like shadows inching along the canyon, gray ghosts prowling in the afternoon. Spain thought, I've taught them some respect for gringo shooting. There were only five *bandidos* left, he reckoned; six at most. If he could stall them off for another hour, it might be enough.

Somewhere down the canyon a dying cow bellowed out its agony. Spain uncorked the canteen and put it to his parched lips. This was the second day of strict water rationing. Or was it the third? He wasn't sure. Had Fred Jeddy died face down in the Río Pantano yesterday or the day before?

That was when a marauding band of Yaqui insurgents had spotted the Roman Six herd trailing toward Arizona. There'd been no more than eight or ten of them all told, but the loot-hungry rebels were eager to fight for so rich a prize. Spain grimaced, recalling how it had been with Tennant and Jeddy helping him fight a rear-guard action while Burl Shambrun, Joe Pratt, and Gus Jubal choused tired cattle northward. Tennant had got his, high in the chest, this morning.

The stink of cow carcasses came to Spain

as he focused tired eyes on a heat-hazed blur of movement down the canyon. He caught a bandoleered raider in his sights; he fired and heard the man screech as he fell.

For a time there was no sign of movement, no sound save the monotonous bleat of the crippled cow. The remote complaint reminded Spain of the many cow carcasses that marked this misery trail from the Río Pantano. More than half the herd was gone.

In this interval of patient waiting, Spain mentally discarded the wondrous dream that had brought him to a heat-hammered canyon in Sonora; the dream that had begun in Texas so long ago. And he remembered an old man who'd once called him a "witless scatterheels." That was the day he'd said good-by to Uncle Bert, the disappointed old lawyer who had raised him and wanted him to continue his schooling.

Spain grinned, recalling that Bert had tried to bribe him with an offer of partnership. But a law office held no appeal for a nineteen-year-old who'd been born on a cow ranch and had a thrusting ambition to acquire a big spread of his own. So he had packed his saddlebags and ridden westward with his dream.

During the footloose years, while he made horse tracks on many ranges, Clay Spain had absorbed a knowledge of cattle and men and women that he could have gained in no other way. He learned how to take care of himself in the awful panic of night stampedes; he matured in the hard-case environment of cow camps and trail-town saloons; he acquired a realistic attitude toward life, understanding that men were neither all good nor all bad, but a mixture of both, and that women were as God made them — women. But through it all he held fast to his dream. Finally deciding that Mexico was the best place to obtain a big spread in a short space of time, he had organized the pooler outfit two years ago.

As he thought about it now, Spain's heat-cracked lips fashioned a self-mocking smile. He hadn't missed by much. "By a goddamn revolution," he muttered. Considering what it had cost two of his partners, he felt fortunate to be alive.

Green-bellied flies swarmed on Tennant's sprawled body; they were a moving cluster on his bloodstained mouth. Spain cursed, knowing there could be no grave. But he thought, Makes no difference to Dan now.

Why, Spain wondered, had Dan spent his last few moments of life arranging for a woman to inherit his worldly goods? What was there about Lace Fayette that had made

Dan's eyes brighten at the thought of her, even when he was dying?

Spain shook his head, wholly baffled. Women, he reasoned, ran pretty much to the same pattern. Especially the pretty, well-made ones. They might have black or brown or blonde hair, and differ in the way they played up to a man. They might be bold or shy, easy to grab or hard to catch, depending on the time and place and how they felt about a man. But underneath, where it really counted, they were all alike, all female. Dan Tennant was old enough to know that. Hell, he'd been around. Spain smiled, remembering one wild night in El Tanque when Dan and Gus Jubal had battered one another to bloody hulks fighting over a swivel-hipped dancer who had finally decided she would spend the night "weeth Señor Spain."

Sodden with fatigue, Spain closed his aching eyes. He thought, To hell with Lace Fayette, and slumped against the rock reef, wholly relaxed. But his ears remained attentive, so that the sound of a dislodged stone falling into the canyon jerked him alert instantly. Squinting his eyes into focus, Spain scanned the heights. It didn't seem possible that a horse could find footing on those steep slabs of almost perpendicular roof, yet he had heard a stone tumble into the canyon.

"Odd," Spain mused, and wondered if he had imagined it.

An unseen marksman down the canyon fired three spaced shots, the slugs kicking up dust a dozen yards short of the reef. Then a bullet whined past Spain's head from above. Spain peered along the east wall and presently glimpsed a puff of gun smoke diagonally across the canyon, where a man had climbed to a high ledge. Changing position now, Spain fired methodically. But the sniper was hidden in a brush-fringed crevasse and made no target at all.

Spain reloaded the Winchester while successive slugs struck the reef so close to him that rock splinters spattered onto the brim of his flat-crowned Texas hat. He thought, I've got to pull out, and he was turning to leave when a bullet burned through his left arm above the elbow.

Down on his belly, Spain looked at the raw meat of the wound. His arm was numb. It didn't hurt, but now, as the blood came, nausea clawed at his stomach. "I'm crippled," he muttered, having a queerly urgent need to express this shocking realization. "The son-of-a-bitch crippled me!"

Spain stuck the useless arm into the

waistband of his pants and drew the belt tight. The thought came to him that he needed a tourniquet, but there wasn't time now. Dragging his Winchester, he crawled toward the sorrel horse.

Blood ran down Spain's arm and made a warm wetness against his belly. He was panting and drenched with sweat when he got behind the ledge where his horse was. It took all his strength to shove the Winchester into its saddle scabbard and then tighten the cinch. His clumsy, one-armed attempt at mounting made the sorrel shy away.

"Stand, son," Spain coaxed, and he stroked the gelding's flank. "We got to go yonderly."

Hearing the sound of hoofs behind him now, Spain turned to see massive Burl Shambrun come down the canyon at a gallop.

"About time some of you galoots showed up," Spain called.

"We've got 'em all through the pass," Shambrun announced, his heavy cheeks dripping sweat.

"Watch yourself," Spain warned. "Those bastards are close."

Shambrun rode up to the ledge; he said smilingly, "The herd is heading for Cartridge Creek. You and Dan come on."

Spain motioned toward Tennant's body. He said, "Not him," and ducked as a bullet caromed off the ledge. He didn't know Shambrun was hit until the big rider fell off his horse.

Shambrun lay motionless. His roan horse shied away, nickering in confusion as another burst of firing racketed along the canyon. The frightened roan trotted toward Spain's horse, head and tail high; he was like that when a bullet hit him. His forelegs buckled as if he had been tripped; he threshed momentarily and loosed a shrill nicker and died.

Spain thought Shambrun was dead too, but now the big man opened his eyes and said in a shocked, disbelieving voice, "I'm bad hurt."

Spain saw blood where a bullet had ripped across Shambrun's shoulder. He drew his pistol and fired two ineffectual shots at the high-perched sniper. "We've got to get out of here quick," he said. "They'll start closing in."

He picked up Shambrun's hat, placed it on the big man's bald head. "Come on," he urged.

Shambrun looked up, his eyes bugging wide with astonishment as he said, "I can't."

Spain cursed, dreading the chore of help-

17

ing Shambrun onto the sorrel and knowing how Burl's added weight would slow the tired gelding. He got his good arm around Shambrun and said savagely, "You've got to do some of it, Burl. I can't do it all."

"No feeling in my arms," Shambrun announced. He thought about that for a moment while Spain crouched beside him, panting and spent. Then, with pure panic dilating his eyes, Shambrun blurted, "I'm paralyzed, by God! Paralyzed!"

Spain thought dully, Bullet must've hit his spine. He made another attempt to get Shambrun off the ground, but the dead weight of Burl's body was too much for him.

"No use," Shambrun muttered. He looked at Spain's holstered gun. He said, "Those Yaquis might drag me to an anthill."

Spain shrugged. There was a throbbing ache in his wounded arm now; when he stood up he felt giddy and so weak he could scarcely pull himself into the saddle. There was a reeling moment in which the canyon seemed to spin around him.

Shambrun's eyes were closed and blood trickled from one corner of his mouth, but now he said, "They'll cut me, Clay. That's what they'll do. And then they'll anthill me."

Spain cursed and tried not to think about it. But because most of his twenty-nine years had been spent on the border, he understood what would happen if they took Burl alive. Yaqui vengeance wouldn't leave it all to the ants; there were certain slow, infinitely deliberate alterations that preceded a victim's final torture. Knowing what Shambrun wanted, and hating him for wanting it, Spain said, "Nothing I can do."

He was turning the sorrel away when Shambrun cried, "You can shoot me, Clay!"

Burl's eyes bulged with the awful pressure of his dread. His face was wet with sweat. "You'd do that much for a dog," he sobbed. "That's all I ask — just what you'd do for a goddamn dog!"

Then, as if a Yaqui knife were already slicing his flesh, Shambrun's voice rose in a frantic high-pitched scream. "Please," he pleaded. "Please!"

Spain drew his gun. He said flatly, "All right, Burl," and fired one well-aimed shot.

Afterward, riding up the canyon at a floundering lope, Spain remembered the dread in Shambrun's eyes, the clawing panic that had made the big man's voice go high and thin and quavering, like a woman's.

Comparing him to Dan Tennant, Spain thought how much better it had been for Dan, who'd died thinking about Lace Fayette. Dan had talked of a woman and died like a man. But poor Burl had thought about being emasculated and so he had screamed like a woman. . . .

The raiders saw Spain now, and rifles began blasting. He heard spent bullets bounce off rock behind him. He thought, They know the herd is gone, but they want me.

The canyon trail was steeper here, a series of tilted slab rock benches that rose to a narrow pass beyond which was the Arizona line. Afternoon's slanting sunlight left a band of shadow along the west wall, but the heat was undiminished. It sucked moisture from Spain's shirt and crusted the soapy lather on the sorrel's sweat-stained neck. Spain peered at the narrow slot of the pass and wondered if his horse would keep going long enough to reach it.

The sorrel did, so near to foundering that Spain dismounted at the first rock outcrop that offered protection. Tying the exhausted horse to a clump of manzanita, Spain unsheathed his Winchester and placed it on a shoulder-high escarpment at one side of the trail. Weak as he was, Spain accomplished a croaking exultant challenge: "Come and get me!" he yelled.

The insurgents probably didn't hear him,

for they had halted nearly a quarter of a mile down the canyon. But they saw him. And they understood that one man could hold off a regiment here; even a crippled man whose bloodshot eyes didn't focus properly.

There was a long interval of waiting during which Spain cut a saddle string and tied it above the wound in his arm, using his teeth to draw the knot tight. He wondered if the bone was broken, and guessed it was. He thought, I'll have to go see Doc Randall in Hondo.

That reminded Spain of his promise to Dan Tennant, and the woman who was to inherit Dan's share of the herd. A mirthless smile rutted his gaunt cheeks as he thought about Lace Fayette. She must be quite a woman to make Dan talk as he had. Spain wondered if she was blonde or brunette. It seemed odd that she should be a partner in the remnants of his pooler herd when he didn't even know what she looked like. Or even what she did for a living. If Dan had told the truth about her staking him, she must be in some sort of business.

She might be the owner of a restaurant or a hotel. But respectable women weren't likely to stake a footloose man.

Was she the proprietor of a dance hall?

Or a brothel?

Well, he'd soon find out, Spain reflected. Hondo wasn't far north of the border. He recalled his last visit there; on a payday, it was, with Lew Wade's foreman trying to talk him out of quitting. Thinking back to that time now, Spain smiled. He'd spent the following year in Texas organizing the pooler outfit. After all that time he was almost back where he'd started, and not much wealthier.

A good town, Hondo. There were saloons where a man could slake his thirst with real bourbon, and a barbershop where he could soak himself in a bathtub. And if he felt in the mood, there was Fancy Anne's parlor house in Shiloh Alley. But presently, remembering what lay behind the rock reef, he thought morosely, I'll get stinking drunk.

When Spain saw the *bandidos* ride off down the canyon, he climbed on the escarpment and waved his battered hat and shouted, "*Adiós,* you bastards!"

Afterward, riding through the pass and observing cow dung on the trail, Spain wondered why neither Joe Pratt nor Gus Jubal had come back to help him. Once through the pass, the herd was safe. Thirsty cattle would have headed instinctively toward Cartridge Creek, which skirted the north base of this divide. They wouldn't need to be driven or kept in a compact bunch. So why hadn't Pratt and Jubal turned back to give him a hand?

"Odd," Spain muttered. "Goddamn odd."

Yet even so, with a rising inquisitiveness nagging him, Spain allowed his tired horse to plod slowly. He didn't realize he was dozing until he almost tipped out of the saddle. He remembered an old night-herd trick. Loosening his holster belt to the last hole, Spain looped it around the saddle horn so that it held him snubbed tight to the pommel.

And then he slept. . . .

Chapter Two

The sorrel's eager whinny awoke Clay Spain. For a moment, while his eyes came into focus, he had no realization of where he was; then he saw the campfire and heard Gus Jubal call, "Who is it?"

Spain understood then that the sorrel had brought him to Cartridge Creek. The air was cool here. Must be nine or ten o'clock, Spain reckoned, and he wondered how long he had slept asaddle. As he came into the circle of firelight Jubal asked, "Where's Dan and Burl?" His broad body cast a barrel-shaped shadow on the ground.

"Dead," Spain said. He lifted his holster belt over the horn. As he stepped down Jubal peered at his bloodstained sleeve and said, "You're hurt."

Joe Pratt, a wiry little man whose cheeks bristled with a brick-red stubble of whiskers, placed a coffeepot on the fire's glowing coals, then reached into a rawhide kyack that hung from the limb of a mesquite tree. "I'll fix you some supper," he said cheerfully.

When Spain started to uncinch his saddle, Gus took over the chore, saying, "Go rest yourself by the fire."

"Want a drink of water first," Spain muttered, and started toward the creek.

But Pratt said, "Here's a whole bucket of drinkin' water, Clay."

Spain couldn't understand it. These men hadn't come back to help him, yet now they seemed wholly solicitous of his welfare. Hunkered on his heels beside the fire, Spain tried to figure it out, and could not.

Joe Pratt warmed up beef in a skillet; he said, "We wondered what was keepin' you so long."

"There was a way you could've found out," Spain said.

Pratt peered at him across the fire. "You mean by goin' back?"

Spain nodded.

"Well, you told us to push the herd and keep on pushin' it all the way to Cartridge Creek," the little man explained.

And Jubal said in a mildly amused way, "We just done what you told us, Clay."

It had never occurred to Spain that Gus was capable of sly humor, but he thought now, I'm being funned. . . .

The second cup of black coffee revived Spain. It banished the dull, dozing lethargy; it brought a clarity of perception that made him acutely aware of the ache in his left arm. And it allowed him to evaluate his partners in relation to past observations, so that he understood now why they had remained with the cattle instead of returning to help him. The hope of huge wealth, which had prompted them to join his pooler outfit, was gone. The fabulous dream of a cattle kingdom was dead. All that remained for them was a small herd to be sold.

Spain thought cynically, Less partners, larger shares. It was as simple as that.

"Not more'n five hundred Roman Six cows over there across the creek," Jubal said thoughtfully.

Spain shaped up a cigarette, grimacing at the misery this slight use of his left hand caused. He wondered how these men would react when he told them that Lace Fayette was to inherit Tennant's share of the herd. Pratt might not object, for he was a meek, dull-witted little man; but greed had driven Gus Jubal all the time he'd been in Mexico, and he had disliked Dan Tennant since the night they'd fought over the cantina dancer.

"You reckon we'll have any trouble selling

26

our cows?" Jubal asked.

Spain shrugged. "Depends on conditions. If Lew Wade has plenty of grass, there'll be a market."

"Is Wade the only one that might buy 'em?"

Spain nodded. "Unless things have changed since I was here, he is." Thinking back to how it had been three years ago, he said, "Wade's Boxed W controls seventy-five per cent of Apache Basin graze. He's got line camps all the way to the Mule Mountains."

"Ain't there no small outfits runnin' cattle in this country?" Joe Pratt inquired.

"Used to be some," Spain said. "But all of them together couldn't buy five hundred cows for cash."

Jubal said, "Supposing Wade won't buy our cattle?"

"We'll have to trail them to Tombstone or Benson," Spain said.

Joe Pratt had been doing some figuring; now he announced, "Five hundred divided by three gives us better'n a hundred sixty cows apiece."

"No," Spain said. "They'll be split four ways." Keeping a strict watch on Jubal, he explained, "Dan left his share to a woman in Hondo."

The effect was some different than he'd expected, for Joe Pratt spoke first. "The hell he did!"

Jubal didn't speak for a long moment. His blocky, firelit face retained its habitual expression of stolid indifference. He took a deep drag on his cigarette and allowed smoke to filter from his wide nostrils before asking, "Is the woman his wife?"

"I guess not. Her name is Lace Fayette."

"A nice name," Pratt said. "Sounds like she might be something special." A sheepish smile creased his cheeks as he added, "I got an itch for a woman. You reckon there's any fancy ones in Hondo?"

"At least one," Jubal muttered with sneering truculence. "A trollop named Lace Fayette."

"You know her?" Spain asked.

"No, but I can guess what sort of woman would run with Dan Tennant. Him and his stud-horse ways."

Joe Pratt said hopefully, "I bet she's a whore. One of them big-breasted ones that wears a peekaboo blouse and earrings."

"Quit your goddamn yapping," Jubal commanded. He peered across the fire at Spain, his squinting eyes bright with speculation. "You think it's fair for some trifling female to get a fourth of our cows?" he demanded.

Spain shrugged, and Jubal said wrathfully, "We rode our rumps off getting those cows out of Sonora. I say it ain't fair for a woman to cut down what little we got left to show for two years' hard work. And her not even his wife."

"Don't rawhide me," Spain objected. "It was Dan's idea, not mine."

"But it's you that's telling it," Jubal insisted, his bull-toned voice raw with resentment. "You could've kept your mouth shut if you'd chose and nobody would've knowed the difference."

He flung the remnant of his cigarette into the fire and muttered, "Now we got to feel like thieves just for keeping what's rightfully ourn."

Spain smiled wryly. "Would it keep you awake nights?" Then he said, "Dan Tennant paid for the privilege of giving Lace Fayette his share of the cattle."

"You mean you intend to go through with it?" Jubal demanded.

Spain nodded.

"But what's Lace Fayette to you?"

"Not a thing."

"Then why give her a hundred and some cows?"

"Because that's what Dan wanted."

"But he's dead," Jubal protested. "What

29

goddamn difference does it make to him now? When a man's dead, he's dead. And he's all through with women. They're no use to a dead man."

"You talk too much," Spain said quietly.

"Who's got a better right to talk? I put good money into your pooler outfit, and worked like a greaser for two years. You said we'd be cattle kings — own the biggest spread in all Mexico. Now we end up with five hundred cows and you want to give part of them to a woman."

When Spain remained silent, Jubal asked, "You still intend to go through with it?"

Spain nodded again. Judging the expression in Jubal's eyes, he kept his right hand close to his holster. There had never been much doubt in his mind about the men that had formed Roman Six. Even though they differed in many ways, they all had been marked by a kindred desire for big money. Watching Jubal's scowling face, Spain thought now that this burly Texan had probably wanted it most, and was therefore most disappointed.

Joe Pratt said uncertainly, "Even with the woman takin' Dan's share, we'd get better'n a hundred head apiece."

"About a hundred twenty-five," Spain agreed, not shifting his gaze from Jubal, who now moved so that his holstered gun lay well forward on his thigh.

Pratt got up and replenished the fire. When fresh flames licked at the wood, he said contentedly, "Makes it more cheerful."

Spain thought about Tennant and Shambrun back there in the Barranca Prieta, and he said cynically, "Cheerful like a wake."

"What you mean by that?" Pratt asked.

Spain shrugged. He considered the possibility of going back for the bodies tomorrow. But by then the buzzards and coyotes wouldn't have left much to pack out. Jubal was right about one thing: A dead man had no use for anything, not even a grave.

A hobbled pack mule crossed the circle of firelight on its way to the creek, floppy ears tilting in rhythm to its mincing step. Somewhere up on the divide a coyote lifted a shrill, two-toned voice. After that for a time there was only the sound of nearby horses foraging for grass.

Finally Jubal asked, "Suppose I don't agree to the four-way split?"

Spain had known that question would be asked. It was as inevitable as thunder after lightning. He got to his feet. There was, he believed, only one way to convince a man like Jubal. He said, "You'll agree, because you haven't got the guts to draw against me."

Jubal remained squatting on his heels, held there by a thin wedge of indecision. Anger stained his perspiring, flame-lit face as he teetered between the tugging pressures of rage and caution.

"What the hell?" Joe Pratt demanded, wholly astonished by an abrupt recognition of impending violence.

Spain ignored him. Stepping close to Jubal, he said, "There's a way you might get my share, along with Dan's."

"I don't want it," Jubal said sullenly. "It's just that I can't abide some trollopy woman getting part of them cows."

Spain laughed at him. He said, "You're a fraud, Gus. A greedy goddamn fraud." Glancing at Pratt, Spain asked, "Will you saddle a horse for me, Joe?"

But he kept Jubal in the fringe of his vision, and so saw him reach for his gun.

Acting upon pure impulse, Spain kicked Jubal in the face, then stomped his right arm as Gus fell backward. All this while he was drawing his own gun, while Joe Pratt stood watching in astonishment.

Spain motioned for Pratt to come around the fire; he said, "Put his gun in the kyack, Joe."

The little man hastened to obey. He said nervously, "Don't see why Gus grabbed like that. No reason for him to shoot at you."

Jubal sat up now. He lifted a hand to his battered, bleeding nose. The anger was gone from his face and from his eyes. Dully, in the way of a man not much interested, he looked up at Spain.

"Had enough?" Spain asked.

Jubal nodded, and wiped his nose on an uphunched shoulder.

"Next time you try drawing against me, I'll use a bullet instead of a boot," Spain warned.

"Won't try it again," Jubal muttered. He shook his head and got to his feet. "I must've gone loco."

Edgy now with the ache in his arm, Spain ordered harshly, "Go saddle me a horse. Not the sorrel."

And as Jubal strode off obediently, Spain said to Joe, "I'll take another cup of that coffee."

There was no friendship here, he reflected, no bond of shared danger and desperate survival. Greed was the core of this partnership, and it spawned a dog-eat-dog brutality. Jubal and Pratt weren't concerned about their dead partners. They were thinking about larger shares of the herd, and the pleasure of spending money on some parlor-house bawd. . . .

Presently, when Spain was in saddle, he announced, "I'm going to get this arm taken care of by a doctor."

"What about us?" Pratt asked. "When do we get to visit Hondo?"

"Not till I get back."

"When will that be?" Jubal inquired, his voice very mild.

"Two or three days," Spain said. He observed a speculative interest in Jubal's eyes, and he wondered about it as he crossed the night-shrouded creek.

That kick in the face had made Gus as meek as a man could be, but Spain thought, He hates my guts.

CHAPTER THREE

Cow smell was strong here. The horse veered around lumpy lopsided shapes in the trail. The cattle, made tame by exhaustion, lay unmoving. The weary brutes had come a long, hard way. Most of them were mother cows, many with sucking calves; a few bulls made up the rest of the herd. There had been over a thousand head at the Río Pantano; foundation stock, the breeding base from which a cattle empire might have sprung had Zapata's insurrection failed.

Remembering the speculative way Jubal had watched him leave the campfire, Spain halted his horse and listened for sounds of travel behind him. Gus might choose to settle this tonight; to overtake him before he got to Hondo — before Lace Fayette learned about her inheritance. That, Spain reasoned, would be one way a greedy man could increase his share. If Gus cut him down, there'd be only Joe Pratt to split with.

"Maybe not," Spain mused. Jubal might shoot Pratt and take the whole herd for himself.

Tight with expectancy, Spain listened. He heard a cow's remote bellowing, but that was all. He waited another five minutes, then rode on at a plodding walk, not sure of his exact direction. The bay horse was following a trail, but whether it was the one that angled toward Hondo, Spain didn't know. There had been a time when he could have ridden in darkness here with confidence, but a man lost his feel for a country in three years.

Wondering how long it would be until daylight, Spain thumbed a match to flame, transferred it to his left hand, and pulled out his watch. The hands stood straight up at six o'clock.

"Forgot to wind it," he muttered.

Afterward, estimating the time since he had left the pass, Spain decided it must be around midnight. If this was the trail to Hondo, he should pass Sam Purdy's place along about daylight. That meant breakfast, and remembering Gail Purdy, who kept house for her bachelor brother, he felt a rising sense of anticipation. There was a girl to make a man wonder. Not a girl, exactly, for Gail was all of twenty-four or -five. But she wasn't an old maid, either. Recalling the time he had taken her to a dance in Hondo, Spain chuckled. Sam had driven the wagon, and except for one brief visit to the saloon, had kept a close watch on his sister all evening. Thinking back to that night, Spain dredged up a time-hazed picture of the supple, sorrel-haired girl who had danced with him. Not much of a talker, Gail. More of a listener. She wasn't a ravishing beauty; he had known prettier girls. His strongest impression of her was an inherent tranquillity, an acceptance of things as they were without complaint.

When the trail angled down a long dry wash that seemed familiar, Spain decided he was on the Hondo trail. Some time after that he realized his arm was numb again. He untied the tourniquet. Fearing infection now, he cursed himself for having failed to cleanse the wound back there at the campfire.

A man could lose an arm in a deal like this. He could spend the rest of his life with a useless stump.

Two shots drove a wedge of tumultuous sound through the predawn stillness. They came from somewhere ahead of him. Three more reports pounded across the brush, two of them delayed and of lesser impact. Spain thought, One man with a rifle and another with a pistol.

Drawing his gun from its holster, he peered at the crest of this low mesquite-fringed ridge. There was no sign of movement. He sent the bay ahead and, reaching the north rim, halted again. He could detect no movement on the flats, but presently he heard a remote thud of hoofbeats off to his left, soon fading.

Expecting to hear the sound of a second rider in pursuit, Spain waited. But none came, and that puzzled him. Had the fleeing man cut down his assailant?

The first delicate streamers of impending sunrise crept into the eastern sky while Spain waited. What, he wondered, had caused the shooting? Why had someone started a fight so early in the morning?

Thinking back, Spain recalled no feud or circumstance that might suggest an answer. Apache Basin was a peaceful place; or it had been, three years ago. There was some grumbling from small ranchers who resented Lew Wade's domination of the range, but no real trouble.

It occurred to Spain that he must be near Sam Purdy's place. He thought, Maybe Sam is mixed up in something. But recalling how meek a man Purdy was, Spain discarded that possibility. But someone had put up a fight out there on the flats, and that man might be waiting for another target.

Spain dismounted. Easing himself into the trail's hoof-pocked dust, he listened, but he heard nothing. A gentle breeze came out of the north, cool and faintly scented with wet pine. He thought, Must've been a rain in the Horseshoe Hills, and reached for his Durham sack.

The mere movement of his fingers fashioning the cigarette set up a throbbing ache in Spain's wounded arm, and when he got his cigarette lighted the smoke tasted rank. This, he reflected morosely, was what ambition got a man: the chance to sit on a lonely trail at dawn with an aching arm, with an unknown gunman ahead of him and Gus Jubal behind him. Gingerly fingering the wound, he thought he detected heat in the blood-crusted flesh around it, and a slight swelling.

The possibility that Doc Randall might have to amputate made Spain sick at his stomach. He said, "Easy money," smearing the words with contempt. Whatever he got for his share of the herd would be the hardest money he had ever earned.

It seemed like a long time until daylight

came. When the Horseshoe Hills took definite shape against the dissolving gloom, Spain climbed wearily into the saddle. Peering at the obscure land ahead, he glimpsed a windmill, and took comfort in the thought that he would be at Purdy's place within a matter of minutes. A cup of hot coffee might diminish the nagging sense of depression. He wondered if Gail was still keeping house for Sam.

He was off the ridge and crossing a sandy wash close to Purdy's front gate when a voice called sharply, "Stop right there!"

Spain halted the bay. He peered at a greasewood thicket to the left of the gate and glimpsed a rifle barrel protruding. He called, "It's me, Sam — Clay Spain."

The door of Purdy's log house opened now and Spain saw Gail step out to the stoop. She peered across the yard for a full moment before saying, "That's Clay Spain, Sam. Don't you remember him?"

Purdy came out of the thicket, a tall, tousle-haired man garbed in bib overalls. Seeing the hostility in his eyes, Spain said, "You look downright proddy, Sam."

"What you doing here?" Purdy demanded, keeping the Winchester raised in front of him.

"Why, I'm waiting for an invite to breakfast."

"You riding for Lew Wade again?" Purdy asked.

Spain shook his head.

"Then what you doing here?"

"On my way to Hondo."

"From where?"

"Sonora. South of the Río Pantano."

While Purdy absorbed that information, Gail called, "Come have some coffee, Clay."

Spain smiled at her, liking the womanly picture she made, the calm friendliness of her invitation. Sam was upset and spooky, but not Gail. Nothing, Spain thought, would rile her much. She was like deep water, revealing no turbulence on the surface. He tipped his hat and said, "Thank you, ma'am," and dismounted.

Leading his horse to the gate where Sam Purdy stood, Spain asked, "You expecting trouble?"

"Already had it," Sam muttered. "Somebody turned loose ten head of steers I had penned behind the barn."

Glancing at Spain's bloodstained sleeve, he asked, "You been shot?"

"Over in the Barranca Prieta yesterday. Zapata's *bandidos* didn't want me to leave."

Purdy unsaddled the bay for him, and

presently, as Spain washed in the basin on the stoop, Gail called, "It's ready."

Sniffing the fine breakfast smell as he entered the kitchen, Spain said gustily, "Bacon and eggs!"

It was characteristic of Gail that she didn't mention his arm as she put a pan of water on to heat and fetched dish towels for washing and bandaging the wound. When her preparations were complete she said, "Take off your shirt, Clay."

She did the job thoroughly and efficiently while Spain ate his breakfast and listened to Sam Purdy's surprising revelations.

"Apache Basin has gone haywire," Purdy said. "The Hondo newspaper got folks excited about irrigating the flats west of town and the bank offered to stake any man who'd join the deal. I kept out of it until they promised to run a ditch down this way. Then I signed up. That's why my steer pen was raided."

"What's that got to do with the irrigation deal?" Spain asked.

"Those ten steers were going to be sold in town to pay my membership into the Hondo Water Association. Now I'll have to gather 'em again, which may take some doing."

It didn't make sense to Spain. "You mean somebody turned your steers loose just because you want to join the Association?"

Purdy nodded. "It's happened to others. Every man that's signed up has had something happen. Busted fences, run-off stock — anything to keep him upset and broke."

"Who's doing it?" Spain asked.

"No proof, but there's only one man against the irrigation project."

"Lew Wade?"

Purdy nodded. "It would cut down the flow of Cartridge Creek to his north range."

"So," Spain mused. "Is Ed Kenyon still sheriff?"

Purdy nodded again. "But Ed can't do anything until someone is caught in the act." The frown ruts on his gaunt cheeks deepened and he added morosely, "Boxed W's big crew has helped elect Ed for the past ten years. Maybe he doesn't want to catch anyone."

Gail had the bandage tied now and was fashioning a sling. Spain asked, "Do you think it's infected?"

"Some," Gail said. A slanting shaft of early sunlight burnished her hair to copper; it made shadows that emphasized her high cheekbones and the long sweet curves of her lips. She placed his arm in the sling, saying, "You should go to Doc Randall right away."

43

Spain nodded agreement. He said, "I'm much obliged," and sensing how inadequate that was, he added, "You're a first-class nurse for sure."

A faint smile altered Gail's cheeks, and now Sam said, "You should see Sis doctor a hurt horse or a sick calf."

The tone of his voice and the expression on his face surprised Spain. He hadn't supposed there was any pride in Sam Purdy, who had seemed humble in all his ways. But there was a bright shining in Sam's eyes as he looked at his sister and announced, "There ain't another girl in Apache Basin that's got her knack with animals."

That seemed to embarrass Gail. She said quietly, "You shouldn't brag about a thing that's natural, Sam. It's just a knack I was born with." Sitting down to eat now, she asked, "Did you go to Mexico like you planned, Clay?"

Spain nodded. "My pooler outfit did all right until Emiliano Zapata busted things wide open."

She hadn't seemed much interested in his plans three years ago, but now she asked, "Are you going to stay in Apache Basin for a while?"

Something in the way she looked at him stirred an old wonder in Clay Spain. Her

44

voice seemed wholly casual, without intimacy, but there was a frank interest in her blue eyes and a womanly warmth that made him wonder how it would be to hold her in his arms. Not on a dance floor, with her brother watching, but alone in some secluded place. . . .

Spain shrugged. "Don't know what I'll do," he said, and heard horses come across the yard.

Sam got up at once. Peering through the doorway, he announced, "Lew Wade and Sid Vivian."

"Odd that they should come here this morning," Gail murmured. But she didn't get up.

Remaining at the table with her, Spain looked out the window and had a slanting view of the two men as they stopped in front of the stoop. They made an odd pair. Wade, freshly shaved and neatly garbed in a white shirt and buff-colored riding pants, said pleasantly, "Good morning, Sam."

In contrast to Wade's habitual graciousness, Sid Vivian merely nodded a wordless greeting. The big-boned ramrod wore a faded cotton shirt and soiled Levis. Whereas his plump-cheeked employer seemed soft and a trifle fat, Sid was beef solid. There was no humor in his bleached-blue eyes;

45

against the stained-oak darkness of his slab cheeks they seemed colorless as shell ice.

Peering at Purdy now, he demanded gruffly, "What's the idea of shooting Lin Graham?"

"Lin Graham?" Purdy echoed. "Was that who I shot at?"

"You didn't just shoot at him," Vivian corrected. "You put a slug in his back."

In the moment of silence now Spain thought, Why is Sid admitting this?

Then Lew Wade furnished an answer by saying, "We had to send him to Doc Randall in a wagon."

Spain understood then why they were here, and wasn't surprised when Vivian announced, "We want to know why you shot a Boxed W man who happened to ride past your place."

It took Sam Purdy a moment to absorb the bold arrogance of that question. Spain glanced at Gail and glimpsed a hint of worry in her eyes; but now, aware of his appraisal, she shrugged and whispered, "You'd think Boxed W owned the whole basin."

Sam said, "I shot at a man who opened the gate of my steer pen. If it was Lin Graham, why was he turning my steers loose?"

"Hogwash!" Vivian scoffed. He glanced at Wade, demanding, "Did you ever hear the

46

like of that?"

Spain couldn't see Wade's face now, for Vivian's horse had edged forward a trifle, but he guessed Boxed W's owner was smiling as he asked, "What possible reason would Graham have for such a silly prank?"

"It wasn't a prank," Sam muttered.

"What do you mean by that?" Vivian demanded.

Purdy said, "I mean it wasn't done for fun."

"Well, if your steers were turned loose, someone else did it," Vivian said with the flat finality of a man accustomed to having his way in all things. "Lin Graham was on an errand to Soledad Spring line camp."

"An unfortunate case of coincidence," Lew Wade said in a blandly regretful voice. "Lin must've been passing at the time someone else tampered with your steer pen."

Sid Vivian made an impatient, chopping motion with his big right hand. "I think it's just a hogwash alibi," he said. "Unless you can prove those steers were turned loose, I'll swear out a warrant for your arrest."

"All you got to do is look," Purdy said. "The sign should be plain enough."

Vivian took off his hat and used an elbow to wipe the sweatband. Bald, save for a monk's fringe of dead brown hair, he appeared bigger and somehow more brutal without the wide-brimmed hat. "We'll take a look," he said. "But there's to be no more shooting at Boxed W riders, regardless. You understand that?"

"Then keep 'em off my place," Purdy said.

Vivian made the impatient, chopping motion again; he warned, "If you shoot at another Boxed W man I'll beat your head off. Keep that in mind."

Then he turned his horse and rode off toward the pen, ignoring Lew Wade, who followed him.

Spain felt sorry for Sam Purdy. He thought, A bitter pill to swallow in front of his sister. Those two men had come here to brazen out an obvious alibi for Lin Graham. They had been forced to make the play because of Graham's need for medical attention, and they'd shoved it down Sam's humble throat.

Gail said wonderingly, "To hear Sid Vivian talk, you'd think he owned Boxed W, instead of Lew Wade."

"Well, I guess that's how Lew wants it," Spain reflected. It occurred to him that he had never seen Wade go anywhere without Vivian, nor had he ever seen him carry a gun. "Wade hires Sid to handle the rough

48

stuff, not being gaited for it himself."

Purdy stood on the stoop until Wade and Vivian rode out of the yard. When he came inside Sam said dully, "I've got the goods on Boxed W, but I still can't prove it." And now, as a delayed sense of resentment engulfed him, he exclaimed, "Sid Vivian has no right to threaten me!"

"Maybe he does," Spain said, and, stepping to the doorway, saw the two men ride westward.

"How so?" Purdy demanded.

"The right of his big fists," Spain said cynically.

Gail asked, "Do you believe that might makes right?"

"Well, it always has."

Gail shook her head. "No," she said, very sure about this. "Might may win, but it doesn't make a thing right."

"I shouldn't have let Vivian talk to me like that," Sam muttered. "Not on my own property."

Gail poured him more coffee. "Don't fret about it," she said gently.

But Sam was fretting. When he lifted his cup his hand trembled. He kept glancing furtively at the doorway, as if expecting Vivian to return.

"I'll help you gather the steers," Gail said.

"There's no rush about it."

Comparing these two people who were so closely related, Spain marveled at the contrast between them. Gail was calm and self-sufficient, accepting what couldn't be helped, and suggesting a constructive course of action. She said again, "Don't fret," and patted Sam's arm.

Sam was at least five years older than Gail, yet now she was mothering him. Spain thought, She's got more gumption than he'll ever have. Watching her clear off the table, he understood that Gail possessed a quality above prettiness. There was in her a woman's capacity for warmth and compassion, an obscure dignity that was something less than pride, something more than humility.

When he picked up his shirt, she said, "I'll fetch you a clean one, Clay."

Spain grinned at Sam. "A poor trade for you," he said. "There's a bullet hole in mine."

"And there'll be patches in the one you're getting," Purdy said without humor. "This is a patchy outfit."

Spain was thinking about that as he went to the corral with Sam. Gail kept the house spick-and-span, but the rest of this place bore the inevitable marks of poverty. Part of the barn's dirt roof had fallen through rotted beams, and the door stood tilted upon one remaining hinge. A plow, its blade rusted from disuse, lay at the edge of a wilted garden, beyond which Spain saw the old furrows of an abandoned alfalfa patch. Even the chickens, which were molting, had a scrawny, hard-scrabble appearance. It occurred to Spain that there were no chickens at Boxed W, or a garden. Like the rusted plow, these were the symbols of poverty.

Watching Sam saddle the bay, Spain felt sorry for this man whose shirt he wore, whose sister had fed and bandaged him. Sam had put up a fight when his steer pen was raided, but he was no fighter, and the need to defend his place had upset him. The knowledge that he'd been in the right hadn't helped any when Sid Vivian threatened him. Sam was the type of man that would always be on the defensive, even when he was right.

When Spain rode from the yard, Gail came out to the stoop and called, "Good luck to you, Clay."

Afterward, riding toward Hondo, Spain thought about her rejection of his cynical philosophy and wondered why her opinion seemed important to him. He had never given much heed to women's opinions. Uncle Bert had always called women a flighty, emotional breed, and Spain had never seen any reason to disbelieve him. "The female mind is a tangled jungle of primitive impulse and passionate reaction," the old lawyer had told him. "Don't ever try to understand the promptings of a woman's mind."

Spain grinned, recalling that though his uncle had remained a bachelor, he had been no recluse where amorous females were concerned. "Romance," Bert had once told him, "is the pure essence of living."

Spain wondered if his uncle were still alive. He hadn't seen him in ten years, or heard from him in over four. During all that time Spain had never regretted his refusal to embark on a legal career, but now, with his big dream discarded and an infected arm aching, he wondered if Bert's scornful declaration had been correct.

Had he been just a "witless scatterheels" ten years ago?

And what was he now?

CHAPTER FOUR

The land here was almost barren of vegetation, being sparsely dotted with tufts of tawny grass and occasional clumps of greasewood; in the morning's bright sunlight the parched earth gave off a metallic shine that hurt Spain's eyes. Riding at a jog trot, he reflected on the perverse notions of the men that had brought plows to Apache Basin, and felt a mild contempt for them. As his horse skirted the southern bulge of the Horseshoe Hills, Spain had an unobstructed view of a far-sprawling plain, beyond which the distance-dwarfed Mule Mountains tumbled eastward into Red Desert's badlands. This was cow country; big-outfit country. It was no place for a man with a plow.

Presently Spain glimpsed a dust plume ahead of him. Watching it, he decided there was one rider approaching from town, and, guessing who it was, he idly wondered about

Sheriff Kenyon's reaction to Graham's shooting. The old lawman, Spain supposed, was on his way to question Sam Purdy, to ask why he had shot a Boxed W rider. Or to arrest him. If Graham died, the charge would be murder.

Thinking of what had happened in the Barranca Prieta yesterday, Spain marveled at the difference a boundary line made. Only buzzards and coyotes were concerned with what had happened over there; but because a man had been wounded near Sam Purdy's place, a sheriff was asaddle to investigate.

As the horses shortened the margin of separation, Spain recognized Kenyon's age-mottled face with its down-swirling sorrel mustache. Ed had been a big man in his prime; now past fifty, he seemed shrunken, as if his weathered old hide was too large for his body, except across a bulging midriff. The glint of a large, gold-plated belt buckle reminded Spain that Ed Kenyon had long ago been the champion roper of Texas; it was the one thing Ed always bragged about after he'd had two drinks at the Shamrock.

When they were almost abreast Kenyon asked, "What you doin' back here, Clay?"

"Got run out of Sonora," Spain admitted with a wry smile. "Those *insurrectos* don't cotton to gringo cowmen." He pulled up beside Kenyon. He took out his Durham sack and asked, "Smoke?"

Ed shook his head, and dug a short-stemmed brier pipe from his shirt pocket. "What's the matter with your arm?"

"Broken, I think," Spain said, and gave his attention to fashioning a cigarette.

"You stop by Purdy's place?"

Spain nodded.

"Did Sam mention any trouble?"

Spain lit the cigarette before saying, "Said he took a couple of shots at a man who turned ten of his steers out of a pen."

That seemed to surprise Ed Kenyon. "Why would Lin Graham do a thing like that?" he demanded.

"Well, Lin works for Lew Wade," Spain said.

"So?"

"Sam seems to think Wade is against the irrigation project."

"What if he is? What's that got to do with turning Purdy's steers loose?"

"Sam seems to think there's a connection," Spain said. Watching Kenyon's reaction to this, he asked, "Whose side are you on, Ed?"

Kenyon scowled at him, resentment riding his voice as he demanded, "What makes you

55

think I'd take sides in a thing like that?"

Spain shrugged, and watching a muscle twitch in Kenyon's right cheek, he observed that Ed had aged considerably in the past three years. His mustache was streaked with gray hairs and his face had a warped flabbiness. Only his deep-socketed blue eyes seemed the same as they had been.

Kenyon said gruffly, "I'm taking no sides, and I want no gossip about it."

Spain grinned at him. "None of my business, anyway," he admitted. "How's your wife?"

"Fine," Kenyon said. "Just fine," and seemed pleased to change the topic of conversation. "You going to stay in Hondo a spell?"

"Long enough to sell some Mexican cows," Spain said. "I've got upwards of five hundred head at Cartridge Creek. You reckon Wade would be in the market?"

"Hard to say. We haven't had a good rain in a year. Just showers in the high hills. But I understand the new railroad that's buildin' through the Whetstones is buyin' lots of beef."

He hadn't filled his pipe, and now he put it back in his pocket. "Got to go have a talk with Sam," he said.

"Don't be rough on him, Ed. Sam

wouldn't hurt a flea, unless it was biting him. You know that."

Kenyon nodded gravely. But he said, "I won't abide shooting. We've had no bad trouble for ten years and there'd be none now if somebody hadn't used a gun."

Then he rode on.

Spain thought about Kenyon's parting words as he jogged toward town. There had been no bad trouble in Apache Basin. But it wasn't just a case of guns. It was because the half-dozen small ranchers knew they stood no chance against Lew Wade's big crew. Men like Sam Purdy, who lacked the power to take what they wanted, were bound to be peaceable. A man could have only what he was capable of holding.

Spain arrived in Hondo shortly before noon. Passing the stock pens at the town's west end, he observed that Main Street seemed unchanged, save for one new building and a sign that said: "HONDO HERALD — Earl Tipton, publisher." Beyond that was the courthouse, the Apache Basin Bank, and Logan's Mercantile, with the Grand Hotel, Slater's Barbershop, and the Wells Fargo office on the opposite side. One long block south of Main Street, and running parallel to it, was Residential Avenue, with its ancient mission and tree-shaded homes.

There was little traffic. A saddled horse stood at the bank hitch rack and a team was pulled up at the Mercantile loading platform. Two men sat on the hotel veranda, and a barefooted Mexican boy with a wood-laden burro came out of Shiloh Alley as Spain turned into it. Riding down this narrow passageway toward the livery stable, Spain glanced at Fancy Anne's parlor house, which was set back between the Shamrock Saloon and Huffmeyer's blacksmith shop. The sagging front stoop and shuttered windows were as he remembered them, but he wondered if the same woman ran the place. Or was there a new proprietor named Lace Fayette?

An old man sat in the stable's wide doorway, above which a weather-tarnished cavalry saber had been nailed and the words "Captain J. B. Ledbetter's Livery" painted long ago. Recalling Cap's talent for inspired recitals about the Confederate Cavalry's accomplishments, Spain gawked at the saber and asked, "What's that cane knife up there for?"

Ledbetter had been dozing. He blinked at Spain, took out a bandanna, and wiped his eyes. Then he said, "That's not a cane knife, friend. It's a genuine cavalry saber, and it's up there to remind folks of the most heroic armed force this country ever bred — Beauty Stuart's Confederate Cavalry!" Recognition brightened his eyes now and he exclaimed, "Why, it's Clay Spain!" He reached up to shake hands; he said, "You're so ga'nted I scarcely recognized you, son."

Spain was uncinching the bay when a man came into the stable and said, "Please hitch up a rig for me, Cap. I'll be back for it in a few minutes."

His precise voice and the correct manner of his dress reminded Spain of a high-school professor who had specialized in expounding Greek philosophy to a class of ranch-reared skeptics. He had the same scholarly expression on his clean-shaved, sensitive face.

"Any news about Lin Graham?" Ledbetter inquired.

"He's still alive," the man said.

As he hurried back down the alley, Cap said, "That's Earl Tipton, editor of the *Hondo Herald,* and a Yankee dude if ever I saw one."

Spain grinned, guessing that the War between the States would never fade in Cap Ledbetter's memory. Watching Cap hang the saddle on a peg, Spain asked, "Do you know a woman named Lace Fayette?"

"Of course I know her. Dare say there ain't a man in this end of Arizona that doesn't."

The warming glint in Cap's old eyes reminded Spain of Dan Tennant; it was the way a man looked when he thought of past pleasures.

"She's a real beauty, and has a good head for business."

Reasonably sure now that Lace Fayette had taken over Fancy Anne's establishment, or was competing with her, Spain asked, "Where can I find this enterprising female?"

"Well, she'll probably be having her noon meal in the hotel dining room about now," Cap said. Leading the bay to a stall, he added, "You can't miss her, Clay. Just look for the loveliest woman you ever saw, and that'll be Lace Fayette."

Walking along the alley, Spain felt a rising sense of anticipation: Dan Tennant must have been right about Lace Fayette. If she could impress an old man like Cap, she must be something special; something a young man should see. But the dull ache in Spain's arm reminded him that his first chore was to visit Doc Randall, whose office was over Slater's Barbershop. As he crossed Main Street he noticed that Earl

Tipton was talking to a woman in front of the bank, and at this same moment the east-bound stage rumbled past on its way to Lordsburg.

Spain nodded a greeting to the barber, who stood in his shop doorway, and, turning to the outside stairway, found it blocked by a redheaded rider who said brashly, "Doc's busy."

"Who are you?" Spain asked, guessing that this was the Boxed W man who'd brought Lin Graham to town.

"Well, if it's any of your business, I'm Red Gillum."

He gave Spain an indolent, disinterested glance and then peered up at the landing in front of Dr. Randall's office as if expecting an important announcement. He was medium tall, his hatchet face burned red by the sun and blotched by brown freckles; the face of a tough, hot-tempered man used to having his own way. He had evidently visited the saloon, for there was a strong smell of alcohol on his breath as he said, "If Lin dies there's goin' to be hell to pay."

"Hell?" Spain prompted.

"You're damned right. No stinkin' sod-buster can kill a Boxed W hand without gettin' hisself strung up to the nearest tree."

"When did you hire on with Boxed W?"

Spain asked mildly.

"Couple years ago. Who are you?"

"A patient to see Doc Randall."

"You can't see him now," Gillum announced flatly. "He's busy."

"So?" Spain mused, revealing no sign of the resentment that flared in him. Gillum, he supposed, considered him harmless because his arm was in a sling. The booze-fired redhead couldn't conceive of anyone's questioning his blockade of the stairway. He was wholly relaxed, wholly confident.

Moving in fast now, Spain slugged Gillum in the belly. Then, as Red doubled over, gasping for breath, Spain hit him hard in the face. He was aware of voices behind him. He heard the barber shout, "Fight! Fight!"

But there was no fight in Red Gillum, who fell against the stairway railing and collapsed with a sigh. Spain bent over and took Gillum's gun from its holster and carried it up the stairs with him. He was at the landing when Doc Randall opened the door. As the bearded medico stepped aside, Spain asked, "You busy, Doc?"

"Of course I'm busy," Randall snapped. "Did you ever see me when I wasn't?"

Spain smiled, remembering what he'd heard about this black-whiskered, fierce-eyed doctor: that he was the gruffest man in Apache Basin and the most tender when it came to caring for women and children.

Glancing at the gun in Spain's hand, Randall demanded, "What's that for?"

"Borrowed it from Red Gillum. He said I couldn't come up here."

"What right has that smart aleck to obstruct my patients?" Doc exclaimed. "I'll put him in his place, by Godfrey!"

As Spain placed the gun on top of Randall's roll-top desk, Doc asked, "What you got in the sling?"

"Maybe a broken arm."

"Bullet?"

Spain nodded, and Randall said gruffly, "Sit down while I go notify the undertaker."

"You mean — Lin Graham died?"

Doc nodded, and motioned toward the screen that formed a partition across the rear of the room. "I thought there was a chance of saving him, but he bled too much. Those fools should've left him at the ranch instead of bouncing him to town in a wagon."

He went out then, and Spain sat down. Guessing what Graham's death would mean, he thought, Sam Purdy is in real trouble. Boxed W's control of Apache Basin was based on the twin pillars of fear and

obedience, and it had been indirectly abet-
ted by Sheriff Kenyon's strict rule against
gun-fighting. Now that control and that rule
had been challenged by the meekest man in
Apache Basin.

Spain shrugged. The politics of this country didn't concern him, one way or the
other. He felt sorry for Sam, and even more
sorry for Gail; but his problem was to sell
five hundred Roman Six cows. And because
Boxed W was his closest market, he could
not afford to get mixed up in this affair at
all.

When the office door opened, Spain
turned, expecting to see Doc Randall's
piratical countenance. But it wasn't Randall.
It was a woman, dark-haired and full-
breasted, the most ravishing woman he had
ever seen. And in this moment, as she
smiled at him, he thought, Lace Fayette!

CHAPTER FIVE

Spain stood up and motioned toward the chair, which she accepted. The faint scent of some delicate perfume came to Spain's nostrils and he observed that her black hair was parted precisely in the middle and drawn back to a tight braided bun at the nape of her neck. The exertion of climbing the stairs had stained her cheeks, and breathing made a measured disturbance at her bosom, where a cameo pendant nestled. Her voice was vibrant with some suppressed emotion, yet low and melodious when she said, "I've something important to ask you."

Spain's surprise must have shown in his face, for she added quickly, "I saw what you did to Red Gillum."

That made no sense to him at all. If this was Lace Fayette, and he felt sure it was, what interest would she have in the slugging of a drunken cowpuncher?

"So?" he prompted.

She smiled at him again. Not brazenly or with flirtatious intent, but with the mild amusement of a woman aware of male consternation. "This will sound odd to you," she warned. "Odd and bold. But I need a man who is not afraid of Boxed W. A man with nerve enough to hit Red Gillum even though he had only one fist to fight with."

Spain grinned, still puzzled. "Red was a trifle careless, and a trifle drunk," he said. Then, because he could scarcely believe that a woman so seemingly cultured and lovely could be a parlor-house madam, Spain asked, "Are you —" and stopped speaking, reluctant to risk using a name that might be an insult if she were someone else.

"I'm Lace Fayette," she said without hesitation. "I'm being very bold about this, but there's not much time. And there's something I need to know."

Spain met her frank appraisal with an equal frankness, liking her brown, gold-flecked eyes and the coarse black lashes that framed them; liking the gentle flare of her nostrils, the firm roundness of her breasts. Looking at her now, Spain understood why Dan Tennant had wanted this woman so urgently, and why Cap Ledbetter spoke of her with an old man's remembrance of past pleasures. She had that power to arouse a man. Without effort, without a gesture of invitation, she stirred a thrusting need in him.

"You haven't told me your name," she said.

"Spain. Clay Spain, fresh out of Sonora. Chased out, in fact."

The name didn't seem to mean anything to her. She nodded and then asked, "Aren't you curious about what I need to know?"

"Some," Spain admitted, increasingly aware of her moist expressive lips, and wondering how it would be to kiss them.

She waited a moment longer before asking, "Are you what you seem to be?"

"What do I seem to be?"

A hint of embarrassment altered her face now, but she said with calm frankness, "What I saw downstairs led me to believe you were a tough drifter. Now I'm not sure what you are."

Spain lifted a hand to his bristled chin as if testing the need for a shave; he glanced at his soiled pants and brush-scarred boots before asking solemnly, "Are you wondering if I'm a dry-goods drummer?"

Lace Fayette laughed. "No, surely not that. But you don't seem quite as tough as you look."

Spain bent over so that his mouth was close to her right ear; very solemnly he whispered, "I'm not."

Doc Randall came in then. The fierceness faded from his eyes as he bowed with agile gallantry and asked, "What can I do for you, Lace?"

"I came up to see Mr. Spain," she said. "May I talk to him while you take care of his arm?"

"If you don't mind seeing him shirtless," Doc agreed.

It occurred to Spain that these two weren't considering his feelings in the matter at all; that he was merely a patient, without dignity or opinion. Taking off his shirt, Spain was aware of his sweat-stained underwear; he said self-mockingly, "I could use a change of clothing."

Lace Fayette didn't speak until Doc began unwrapping the bandage. Then she asked, "Would you be interested in a job, Mr. Spain?"

"What kind?" he asked.

She glanced at his holstered gun and said soberly, "As a guard, protecting Sam Purdy."

That puzzled Spain. Why should the proprietor of a parlor house want to hire a bodyguard for a two-bit rancher?

It didn't seem possible that this voluptuous woman could be in love with so meek and colorless a man. Yet what other reason could there be?

Doc had the bandage off now and was examining the wound. Spain asked, "Is there much infection?"

"Quite a bit."

Spain eyed the wound with swift apprehension; he asked flatly, "Too much?"

Randall probed the discolored flesh. He squeezed the puckered wound between thumb and forefinger. Finally he said, "Cauterizing should fix it."

A gusty sigh slid from Spain's lips. He grinned at Lace Fayette and asked, "What's your interest in Sam Purdy?"

"Why, the interest any banker would have," she said.

"Banker?"

Lace Fayette nodded. "The Apache Basin Bank. I inherited it from my uncle two years ago."

Spain eyed her in astonishment. "A lady banker?" he asked in a disbelieving voice.

She nodded. "My bank has made loans to most of the small ranchers in the basin, including Sam Purdy."

"But what's that got to do with this gun-guard proposition?" Spain demanded.

"I heard what Red Gillum said as he rode

69

off to report the news of Lin Graham's death," she explained. "He said the Boxed W crew would lynch Sam Purdy."

Doc Randall said, "Wouldn't surprise me much if they did. This is the first time anyone ever stood up to that high-binding outfit."

"That's just it," Lace Fayette said urgently. "That's why it's so important that nothing should happen to Sam Purdy. If he's hurt in any way, the others will never stand up for their rights. They'll go on bowing to the will of Lew Wade. But if Purdy is allowed to stand trial in court, where he's sure to be exonerated for protecting his own property, then the others will take heart and there'll be a chance for the Hondo Water Association to survive."

Hearing the vibrant tone of her voice and observing the glow that warmed her gold-flecked eyes, Spain thought, It's not Sam she's interested in. This woman's passionate interest wasn't prompted by romantic desire or a woman's need for attracting male attention. It might be fired by some deep-rooted resentment toward Boxed W, or by an ambition to build an irrigation project, or by a combination of both those elements.

So thinking, he asked, "Then it isn't just Sam Purdy?"

70

"Of course not," she said with a trace of irritation. "It's for the change that will benefit all Apache Basin."

"Except Lew Wade," Spain said.

"That smiling aristocrat," she scoffed. "He and his brute foreman have run this country so long they think they own it."

"They probably believe what the Sophist told Socrates," Spain said. "That might is right, and justice is the interest of the stronger."

That seemed to surprise Lace Fayette. She said, "So you're more than a tough drifter." Then she added thoughtfully, "I choose the passage in Plato that says that while the weak suffer what they must, the strong do what they can. You are strong. Will you do what you can?"

"How about Sheriff Kenyon?" Spain asked. "He's the one that should protect Sam."

Lace Fayette shrugged. "Ed Kenyon is an old man," she said. As if reluctant to say this, she added, "I believe he's afraid of Sid Vivian."

"No," Doc disagreed. "Ed isn't afraid. It's — well, it's something besides that."

Spain winced as Randall cauterized the wound. When that was finished he asked, "Is the bone broken?"

"May be nicked a trifle, but there's not enough swelling for a fracture."

As Randall dressed the wound, Lace Fayette asked, "Will you take the job?"

"You mean guard Sam until he's safe in jail?"

She nodded.

Spain considered the fact that he wanted to sell his herd to Lew Wade, and the long drive that would be necessary if he had to sell elsewhere. Finally he said, "Reckon I owe him that much."

"You owe Sam?"

"For the shirt I'm wearing, and a good breakfast." Then, remembering Tennant's request, Spain said, "You've inherited about a hundred and twenty-five cows. Dan Tennant's share of the Roman Six herd at Cartridge Creek."

"I inherited them? You mean Dan Tennant is dead?"

Spain nodded. "He died on the way out, along with two other pool partners. He wanted you to have his share of the cows."

"Poor Dan," she said softly, her face grave. "He had such high hope for success in Mexico."

Recalling how Dan had talked about this woman, Spain said slyly, "That wasn't his only hope."

Lace Fayette's gold-flecked eyes met his directly. Some secret knowledge brought a faint stain of color to her cheeks; but now, as she rose and stood before him, she was wholly self-possessed. "Dan Tennant owes the bank five hundred dollars and some interest," she said. "If that much is available after his cows are sold, I'll accept it." She turned to the door and opened it, then asked, "Will you watch out for Sam Purdy?"

Spain nodded, and watched her leave. "A lady banker," he mused.

"The most unusual banker you'll ever meet," Doc Randall said. "She lends money to every short-staked man that asks for it. Odd thing is she usually gets paid in the long run. Like your friend Tennant."

As he finished with the bandage he reflected, "She's the direct opposite of her uncle, who wouldn't lend a dollar to a poor man without having ten dollars' worth of security. John Holt took his risks with the big boys like Lew Wade. At one time he owned a half interest in the Crystal Palace at Tombstone, and backed a place in Galeyville. But Lace lends money to the little fellows."

"She's quite a woman, too," Spain said.

Doc nodded. He said, "You owe me two dollars." As the undertaker came in with an assistant, Doc growled, "About time you got here."

Sheriff Ed Kenyon got into the saddle with an old man's regard for stiff joints. He smiled at Gail Purdy, saying, "Much obliged for the coffee." Then his face turned grave as he said to Sam, "If Lew Wade swears out a warrant, I'll have to arrest you."

Purdy nodded acceptance of that. "No jury would convict a man for doing what I did," he muttered.

"You can't tell what a jury'll do," Kenyon said. "Especially about a killing. If Lin Graham dies, you'll be in trouble, son. Bad trouble."

"Well, what's a man supposed to do?" Purdy demanded. "Just sit and watch his steers turned loose?"

Ed Kenyon thought about that for a long moment before saying, "Nobody would believe Graham intended to steal those steers."

"Then why did he turn 'em loose?"

"Can't figure it out," Kenyon admitted. "I'm going to have a talk with Lew about that. I'm going over there right now."

Gail called from the doorway, "Perhaps you should talk to Vivian, Sheriff. He acts as if he's the boss."

"Just his way," Kenyon said. "Sid talks big, but he's only a foreman working for wages." He contemplated Gail thoughtfully; he asked, "Has Lin Graham had notions about you?"

"Notions?"

Ed smiled. "The kind a man gets about a pretty girl," he explained.

Gail didn't answer, but Sam said angrily, "He kept pestering Sis to go to a dance with him. Wouldn't take no for an answer, so I told him to quit fussing at her."

"That might explain why he turned your steers loose," Kenyon suggested. "Maybe he just did it for spite."

He rode out of the yard then, and turned west. Watching him, Sam said morosely, "I'm not going to jail, Sis. I'll take to the hills first."

"But that wouldn't solve anything," Gail objected. "You'd be a fugitive from justice, and the whole Boxed W crew would hunt you."

Sam grimaced. But he said stubbornly, "I can't abide the thought of being in a cell."

"It wouldn't be for long, Sam. Just until your trial's over." Then, with swift enthusiasm, she added, "Why, it might be for only an hour or so, if Lace Fayette put up your bail. And I'm sure she would."

Sam thought about that. He said, "I suppose she might," and some of the gravity went out of his eyes.

But later, when he saw Red Gillum ride past on a sweat-lathered horse, Sam thought instantly, Graham died.

And he was afraid.

CHAPTER SIX

Clay Spain contemplated his reflection in the Shamrock Saloon's back-bar mirror. His cheeks were a trifle gaunt, he reckoned, but he looked human, now that the black whiskers were gone. He said, "Sure beats hell what a shave, a bath, and some new clothes will do for a man."

It was midafternoon, and the bar was deserted save for Jack Benteen, the middle-aged, darkly handsome proprietor, who asked, "You heard about Sam Purdy killing Lin Graham?"

Spain nodded. He said disgustedly, "The damnedest things happen."

"They do for a fact," Benteen agreed. He swabbed the bar for a moment before adding, "Women sure cause lots of trouble, one way and another."

"What have women got to do with Graham's death?"

"Lin had a case on Gail Purdy, except

when he got drunk. I hear Sam run him off a while back."

"Well, Graham wasn't calling on her at five o'clock in the morning," Spain said. Then he asked, "What difference did his being drunk make?"

Benteen chuckled. "Lin forgot all about Gail Purdy when he got a couple of drinks in him. Have you seen Lace Fayette?"

Spain nodded, and Benteen said, "Then you'll savvy how it was with Lin. Sober, he never mentioned Lace, knowing he didn't have a chance with her. But whenever he got drunk, she was the woman he wanted. It was odd the way he talked about her with the whisky courage in him. He'd brag that she needed a high-powered stud like him — that he was the only man in Apache Basin that could really satisfy a woman. But he always ended up visiting one of Fancy Anne's girls."

Benteen continued to rub the rosewood bar; he said thoughtfully, "It's a queer thing about respectable women. If they're built the way a woman should be, and have a face to go with it, they give a man an awful itch. Worse than the flirty ones."

"Suppose," Spain agreed. According to what the barber had told him about Benteen and Earl Tipton's wife, Jack might be having some woman trouble himself. It was generally understood that Fancy Anne had set Benteen up in the saloon business, and that he was her man. But the barber said Benteen was meeting Mrs. Tipton on the sly.

Cap Ledbetter came in then and said cheerfully, "I saddled your horse, Clay. He's outside at the hitch rack."

"How come?" Spain asked.

"Well, Lace Fayette asked me to do it. She said you'd be in a hurry to leave town."

"Who the hell does she think she is?" Spain demanded.

Cap peered at him as if wholly puzzled. "What you mean by that?"

Benteen seemed to understand Spain's resentment, for he explained, "Lace is used to having her way in Hondo. She's done so much for folks, lending money and pointing out things that need doing." The saloon-keeper smiled wryly, adding, "I think she's the one that influenced Earl Tipton to run an editorial against Fancy Anne's place. He called it the Gomorrah of Apache Basin and got the ladies on Residential Avenue all worked up about it."

"She's a great one, that Lace," Cap said. "She'll make Hondo the garden spot of

Arizona one of these days. Just wait and see."

Spain's resentment had dissolved while they talked. Just thinking about Lace Fayette stirred a sense of anticipation in him. He finished his drink and, recalling the barber's gossip, thought amusedly, Earl Tipton denounces Fancy Anne's parlor house while his wife honeyfusses Fancy Anne out of her man.

His amusement must have shown, for Benteen asked, "Something comical occur to you, Clay?"

Spain chuckled. "Comical as hell."

"Secret?"

"Well, not exactly," Spain said, and went out to his horse. An odd world, he thought; a mixed-up mess for a fact.

When he rode out of Shiloh Alley, Lace Fayette stood in the bank doorway. She beckoned and walked out to meet him on the sidewalk. Standing there in the afternoon sunlight, she was what Dan Tennant had called her: a woman; not a girl, but a beautiful full-blown woman.

"Earl Tipton just got back from Purdy's place," she said urgently. "He thinks Sam may hide out in the hills, which is the worst thing he could do. Tell Sam I'll furnish bail — that he won't be locked up at all."

"Did Ed Kenyon come back?" Spain asked.

"No, he went on to Boxed W. I wish you'd hurry, Mr. Spain."

"The first name is Clay," he said.

"Yes, and you may call me Lace," she agreed. "I wish you'd bring Sam to town before Wade's tough crew does something to him."

"Suppose Sam doesn't choose to come?"

"Bring him anyway," she said confidently.

Spain thought about that for a moment; he said, "Sounds a trifle highhanded to me."

"But it's for his own good," she insisted.

"What difference does that make? I've still got no right to force him."

Lace regarded him with frank speculation, twin dimples forming in her cheeks as she smiled and said, "So you believe the weak have certain inalienable rights, regardless of what the Sophist said to Socrates."

Spain shrugged, and she said earnestly, "Sam will be safe in town. He can stay at the hotel until his trial is over. By that time Lew Wade and everyone else will understand that Boxed W can no longer control Apache Basin."

She made it sound right and reasonable, and now, as she asked, "Will you do it, Clay?" he had no defense against the things her brown eyes did to him.

"Sam will come to town," he promised, and rode on out of Hondo. But afterward, crossing the southern slope of the Horseshoe Hills, Spain felt less confident. What right had he to tell Sam Purdy what to do? And why should he?

"None of my damned business," Spain told himself, and marveled at the ease with which Lace Fayette had involved him in something that didn't concern him at all. He should be heading for Boxed W to make a deal with Lew Wade for the Roman Six herd. That was his business, and he should be attending to it instead of running damned-fool errands for a lady banker. Gus Jubal and Joe Pratt wouldn't sit on their rumps at Cartridge Creek forever. He smiled, remembering Joe's eager announcement that he wanted a woman. He thought, Maybe that's what's ailing me.

Disgusted now, Spain decided he would tell Purdy about the bail offer and leave the rest up to him. If Sam wanted to come to town, well and good; otherwise, to hell with it. Sam had a right to make his own decisions.

Spain moved his left arm up and down, testing it. There was some soreness, but the ache was gone. His thoughts kept returning to Lace Fayette. Even her name fascinated him. Lace. It made a man think of intimate feminine garments, revealing and sweet-scented.

Spain shook his head. "Romantic fever," he muttered. "I've got it bad."

It was dusk now, and lamplight made its yellow beacon in Purdy's yard. Spain wondered if they had eaten supper, and hoped they hadn't. He was almost to the gate when he heard Gail cry, "Don't! Please don't!"

And as he turned into the gateway he heard Sid Vivian's caustic voice demand, "Are you leaving Apache Basin tomorrow like I said?"

Then Spain saw them in front of the house. Red Gillum had Sam's arms locked behind him while Vivian stood with both fists cocked; a third man held Gail on the stoop.

Sam's lamplit face revealed blackened eyes; his nose and mouth were bleeding. He cried, "You've got no right —"

Vivian clouted him in the face. "I'll show you who's got a right!" he growled.

Spain thought resignedly, I'm too late, and took some comfort in the reflection that they didn't seem to intend to hang Sam.

"Are you pulling out tomorrow?" Vivian demanded, his bleached-blue eyes shining as he waggled blood-smeared kunckles an inch from Sam's punished face.

"Don't hit him again!" Gail pleaded.

Without turning to look at her, Vivian said harshly, "Tell your brother to make up his mind. No man shoots a Boxed W rider and stays on in Apache Basin."

Red Gillum complained, "I still think we should string him up."

"I'll do the thinking," Vivian muttered, and struck Sam a vicious chopping blow that broke his nose.

Sam's whimper of pain spurred Gail to a desperate struggle against the man that held her. "Let me go to him!" she sobbed. "He's hurt!"

The man laughed. "Sid, you've done hurted poor Sam."

Spain loosed a whispered curse. A man shouldn't butt into a thing like this; but now, as Vivian struck again, Spain drew his gun and called sharply, "That's enough!"

Halted in darkness beyond the doorway's shaft of lamplight, he had them at a disadvantage. "First man moves gets a slug in the gut," he warned.

Vivian peered toward him and demanded, "Who are you?"

Ignoring that, Spain said, "Turn him

loose, Red. Step clear so I can see your right hand."

At that instant, as Gillum released Sam, Spain caught a blur of movement on the stoop. The man there swung Gail around in front of him so that she made a living shield; he held her snug with one arm and drew his gun.

"Git him, Bob!" Gillum yelled, not grabbing his own gun.

Gail struggled frantically, pulling Bob off balance as he fired, the bullet going so wild it barely missed Vivian.

"No! No!" Sid shouted.

But Gail fought clear of her captor and Spain had a fleeting target. He fired as Bob darted off the stoop into darkness; at the same instant Vivian and Gillum whirled out of the lamplight.

Spain fired at the vague shadow of Gillum's moving shape, then yanked his horse into a turn. He was hastily dismounting when a bullet knocked the bay into floundering motion. As Spain stepped down, the horse staggered against him with an impact that drove Spain to his knees; then a second bullet struck and the horse went down.

Moving clear of the bay's wild threshing, Spain collided with a windmill watering trough. Guns blasted as he crouched behind the low barrier.

Spain saw Gail guide Sam onto the stoop. Sam held one palm over his nose; he walked in the uncertain, knee-sprung way of a man dazed and in pain.

The guns were silent now, but Spain made his guess as to their approximate location. Red and Bob, he believed, were at the corner of the house, or near it. Sid Vivian was off to his right somewhere. For a brief interval, while Gail helped Sam into the house and closed the door, there was no sound in the yard. Then, as the light went out, Gillum called, "Where you at, Sid?"

Vivian didn't answer.

Sid was too smart for that, Spain thought. Sid's instinctive reaction was to keep himself hidden and wait in silence until the time was right. Unhampered by conscience, he acted with a feral savagery. Courage, bravery, fair play — they were words without meaning to Vivian. Spain smiled, thinking that Sid must be a trifle puzzled about this deal. The Boxed W ramrod couldn't have identified him, and there was no way for Sid to guess who had broken up his punishment play.

Sid would hate his guts for that.

CHAPTER SEVEN

The horse had ceased its threshing. Spain heard a vague rumor of movement across the yard, as if someone were taking a few stealthy steps toward the corral. Gillum called, "Is that you, Sid?"

Spain was tempted to fire toward the voice, but thought better of it. They didn't know his exact location and were afraid to rake the yard with random bullets for fear of hitting one of their own men. It occurred to Spain that he would be much more vulnerable to attack if there were only two guns against him, or just one. As it stood now, they couldn't be sure, and so doubt shackled them.

Spain lay on his side, peering into the quilted darkness. He heard the faint rattle of a curb chain as a horse rubbed its head against a corral post. It occurred to him that there were three saddled horses over there, and Sid Vivian was nearest to them. A gentle breeze set the windmill to slow clanking; the air felt cool against Spain's sweat-dampened face, and it reminded him that summer was almost gone. Presently the breeze died, and now, as the windmill stopped turning, he heard a sound of movement and a low murmur of voices directly east of him. Red and Bob, he supposed, were moving farther away from the house, probably heading toward the gate.

Moments later he heard Bob complain, "I'm bleeding awful!"

Spain thought, So I hit him, and was surprised that one of his snap shots had found a target. He heard the two walk toward the gate, their footsteps quite plain. Presently Red called, "Bring out the horses, Sid. I'll cover you from here."

As if already asaddle and waiting, Vivian rode away from the corral leading a pair of horses. Spain used that disturbance to cover a change of position; he stepped around the trough and cat-footed toward the barn. When those three got together there'd be nothing to restrict random shooting. Spain found the barn doorway and eased inside it. Listening now, he heard Bob's bitter cursing and guessed the wounded rider was having a bad time mounting. Vivian ordered impatiently, "Come on, come on!"

After that there was the hoof tromp of departing horses. Spain waited, guessing that once they were on the trail, Gillum and Vivian would cut loose with their guns and rake the yard with a wild searching fusillade.

But no shots came, and in the continuing silence Gail called urgently, "Are you all right, Clay?"

Spain said, "Yes," and wondered how she had identified him.

"Shall I light the lamp?"

"Not yet," he said, and at that moment bullets shrilled across the yard. One broke a window; another clanged against the plow, ricocheting crazily.

As another bullet broke glass in a window, he fired at a flare of muzzle flame northeast of the yard. The range was too far for his pistol, but the shot pulled Vivian's fire away from the house. Bullets tore through the barn's flimsy boards; a slug ripped the doorway arch and splinters slashed Spain's cheek.

There was a respite while Vivian reloaded, and now Gail came running across the yard's darkness, calling, "Here's Sam's Winchester, Clay. It's loaded."

Spain cursed. "Go back!" he ordered.

But she came on into the barn, insisting,

"You need a rifle, Clay."

Spain took the gun; he said harshly, "Get into a corner and keep down."

Vivian fired again, the bullet missing the barn. Sid waited then, wanting the muzzle flare of a return shot for a target. Spain shot from the south side of the wide doorway and then ducked to the north side. As bullets began smashing into the opposite doorframe, he took deliberate aim at the muzzle flash. Triggering as fast as fresh shells could be levered into the firing chamber, he emptied the Winchester in a continuous burst of firing.

There were no more shots from the trail. For a moment Spain thought he had knocked Vivian from the saddle. But presently he heard a horse lope eastward.

"Have they gone?" Gail asked.

"Yes," Spain said. "This rifle was too reachy for Sid's taste."

A backwash of excitement brought its inevitable reaction. Moments ago he had been shooting and being shot at; now, as the tension drained out of him, he felt spent and depressed. He thought, A loco deal, for nothing had been solved by all the shooting. The realization that it had cost him a good horse increased his sense of futility, and he muttered, "A damned useless deal."

Gail came up to him in the doorway, her face an obscure oval against the barn's blackness. "Not useless," she disagreed. "You saved Sam."

"Saved him, hell," Spain scoffed. "They'll shoot him next time."

She had no answer for that. She stood there, silent and uncertain, until Spain asked irritably, "How about some supper?"

"I'll fix it in a jiffy," Gail promised, and started toward the house. Then she asked, "Do you think they'll come back tonight?"

"No," Spain said. But he wasn't that sure. There was no telling about Sid Vivian. The man was sly as an Apache, and he would choose a time of attack that suited him. There was no false pride in Sid. The setup here hadn't been right for him, and so he had run out on it. But he was committed to the banishment of Sam Purdy, and so he would come back.

When Gail lit the kitchen lamp Spain went over to the dead horse, taking care to keep outside the shaft of lamplight. He pulled his Winchester from the saddle scabbard and stood there with both rifles, tautly listening. The Boxed W trio had headed toward town; Gillum, Spain guessed, had gone ahead with the wounded Bob, while Vivian took his final fling with the rifle. If they had continued on into town, there'd be nothing to worry about for a few hours, at least.

Gail called, "It's ready, Clay."

And at that moment, as he turned toward the house, Spain heard the sound of a rider approaching from the west.

Sheriff Ed, he thought. Kenyon had probably stayed for supper at Boxed W and was now coming to arrest Sam Purdy.

"Supper's ready," Gail called again.

"All right," Spain said, and now, as the rider approached the gate, he asked, "Is that you, Ed?"

"Yes," Kenyon said. "What you doing here, Clay?"

As he came through the gate Spain asked, "Didn't you hear the shooting?"

"I certainly did." Kenyon said, plainly displeased.

"Then you should know what I was doing," Spain muttered, and went on into the house.

At eight o'clock Jack Benteen flipped away the butt of his after-supper cigar and stepped off the hotel veranda. Walking in the leisurely fashion of a man with no specific destination, he passed the *Hondo Herald*'s lamplit doorway and observed Earl Tipton at his desk. Going on to the next corner, he turned southward, crossing Residential Avenue and entering the unlighted alleyway beyond it. Here he waited for a moment, as if undecided. A lamplit window on the second floor of the bank building attracted his attention; the shade was up and he glimpsed Lace Fayette as she moved from sink to kitchen shelves, wiping dishes. An old speculation stirred Benteen's imagination; even at this distance Lace Fayette's way of walking made him wonder about her. It was the one flaw in her voluptuousness, to his way of thinking. Her face, her body, her voice — everything about her fitted the image of a man's desire; but she walked tight-hipped and prissy, like a strict old maid. An odd thing.

Benteen passed two dark back yards and went unerringly to the open gate of the third. Eve Tipton was waiting for him on the back porch, wearing a silk kimono. She said happily, "I hoped you'd come tonight," and drew him down beside her on the old leather lounge that had become their love seat. The scent of her lilac perfume was a familiar fragrance that stirred him now as always, yet he voiced a nagging apprehension: "This is a risky thing for you. Suppose one of your neighbors hears us?"

Eve brought her face against his. Missing

his mouth, she drew moist lips along his cheek until she found it. "Who cares?" she said. "Just so we're together."

Her receptive attitude toward his first advances had hugely fed Benteen's vanity. It wasn't often that a lady from Residential Avenue accepted a Shiloh Alley saloon-keeper on equal terms. But afterward, astonished by his swift conquest, Benteen found his satisfaction submerged in the flood tide of this woman's passionate response. He couldn't understand her. In every way but this she was a cultured and proper lady. What, then, was the reason for these illicit back-porch evenings?

Benteen wanted to believe he was the reason; that the male appeal of him had overwhelmed her. But he knew himself for what he was — a disillusioned man no longer young, whose hair was thinning to baldness; a tramp bartender that had been grub-staked by the proprietor of a bawdy house. Why did this attractive, aristocratic wife, whose husband was younger than he, give herself to him so eagerly?

"You're quiet," Eve said with mild censure. When he shrugged she pulled him possessively against her and asked, "What am I, honey?"

Benteen withheld the answer, knowing

how this delay affected her. It was a ritual in which she did the urging while he teased her with feigned reluctance; a ritual of increasing anticipation for them both.

"Please," she whispered, and nibbled at the lobe of his ear. Her hands fondled him and she coaxed, "Tell me what I am, Jack darling."

There was no light, and he could not see her, but the delicate scent of her body told him the kimono was open. With his lips against the fragrant satin of her bosom he inhaled deeply, for this also was part of the ritual.

Eve squirmed in his embrace; she arched her back so that her breasts pressed hard. "Tell me!" she begged.

"You're my sweet-smelling woman," Benteen told her, now fully aroused and wanting her as she wanted him. . . .

Afterward Eve sighed, "That's worth any risk." When he remained silent, she demanded, "Well, isn't it?"

"Sure," Benteen agreed. "Sure it is."

But he couldn't forget that Fancy Anne suspected him. . . .

A woman in the next yard came out with a lantern and walked to a chicken coop. Eve whispered, "If Mrs. Harlan could only see me now!" and was so amused at the thought that she giggled.

Benteen clamped a palm over her mouth. "Hush yourself," he commanded. When Mrs. Harlan returned to the house, he said, "I'd better go."

"Not so soon," Eve protested, her arms tightening around him. "I've been alone all day, and bored to tears."

"Didn't Earl come home for supper?"

"Yes, and chattered on and on about the piece he's going to write. Something to do with Sam Purdy defending his home against Boxed W. As if I'm interested in that!" She sighed. "Ever since he bought the *Herald* he's been like that. I'm supposed to play second fiddle to a newspaper."

"He seems to be on real friendly terms with Lace Fayette," Benteen said.

"Just business. Earl probably doesn't even know she's good-looking."

"Don't see how he could miss seeing it."

Eve drew back. "Do you think she's prettier than me?"

"Of course not," Benteen lied with Celtic grace.

Eve didn't speak for a moment. Finally she said, "Men are such fools about women. Lace Fayette may be beautiful, but she'd be no great prize for a man to win. That kind never is."

Jealous, Benteen thought, and didn't blame her. Every wife in Hondo was a trifle jealous of Lace Fayette. He smiled to himself, remembering that even Fancy Anne had accused Lace of being a man-teaser. He heard footsteps now and got up quickly, thinking it was Earl; then as a screen door banged at the Harlan house, he loosed a gusty sigh.

Eve hadn't seemed perturbed at all; she laughed at him and asked, "Are you afraid of Earl?"

"Sure," he admitted. "He'd probably shoot me."

That seemed to amuse her. She lay back and laughed; she said breathlessly, "That's so comical — Earl shooting you or anyone else."

"But you're his wife," Benteen insisted. "His sweet-smelling, beautiful blonde wife."

"Well, Earl doesn't seem to know it. Not since he got a newspaper of his own. He's too busy thinking up editorials that will make Hondo a fine, big town to live in ten or twenty years from now."

"A poor way to treat a wife," Benteen sympathized. "Doesn't he know a woman needs to be loved?"

"I guess Earl just doesn't care," Eve said bitterly. She stood up and drew him against her with a strength that astonished him, for she was slim and small-boned. She whispered, "But you do, don't you, honey?"

Benteen kissed her long and hard. He thought, It's not me, and understood that any man would be the same to her.

As if prompted by his thought, Eve said, "I saw a new man in town today. When he rode out of Shiloh Alley, Lace Fayette went out and talked to him."

"What did he look like?"

"Well, he's tall and dark. Sort of handsome in a hard, hungry way."

"Did you notice what color his eyes were?"

"A smoky blue. Almost gray."

Benteen chuckled. "You took a real good look, didn't you?"

She nibbled at his ear. "Jealous?"

Benteen knew that he had guessed right; that a husband's neglect was the reason this warm-blooded wife had accepted a Shiloh Alley suitor. Eve had needed male attention and would probably have been attracted to any man that offered it. He thought, I just happened to be the lucky one.

But afterward, when he walked into Shiloh Alley and a woman called to him from a dimly lighted veranda, Benteen wasn't sure about his luck. Fancy Anne had a temper that went with her red hair.

CHAPTER EIGHT

Coming into the lamplit kitchen, Spain observed how dusty his clothes were. "Look like a ground hog," he muttered, and went back to the stoop to brush himself off.

Sheriff Kenyon dismounted and came across the yard, the silver star on his vest sharply reflecting lamplight. "What was all the shooting about?" he asked.

"Me," Spain said, and stepped into the kitchen.

"Why, there's blood on your cheek!" Gail exclaimed, and came over to examine the splinter scratch, but Spain rejected her solicitude by announcing:

"All I need is food."

As she poured him hot coffee she said, "I'm sorry about your horse."

"My own damned fault," he muttered.

That seemed to puzzle her. She peered at him as if bewildered, and asked, "Are you sorry you interfered, Clay?"

"Well, I'm not exactly tickled about it," Spain said, and when she stood looking at him, he said, "How about letting a man eat in peace?"

She turned abruptly away then, and, seeing Kenyon at the door, invited him to share the warmed-up supper, but Ed said, "Had mine." Then he asked, "Where's Sam?"

Gail told him about the beating, her voice vibrant with indignation. She said, "I think Sid Vivian would've killed Sam if Clay hadn't shown up when he did."

Spain ignored the talk until Kenyon asked, "How'd you happen to come back here, Clay?"

"That's my business," Spain said.

Kenyon didn't like that. He said sharply, "Now listen here, son. Don't take your spite out on me."

"Then quit nagging at me," Spain said.

Sheriff Ed glanced at Gail and shrugged. Finally he said, "Fighting affects some men like that. Makes them meaner'n a gored bull afterward."

Spain finished his first cup of coffee, and Gail was pouring him a second when Sam came out of the bedroom holding a damp, folded towel against his nose. Both eyes were swollen to narrow slits, their purpling darkness emphasizing the pallor of his bruised cheeks.

"You shouldn't be up," Gail protested.

But Sam took a chair at the table and asked, "You here to arrest me, Ed?"

Kenyon nodded. He appraised Sam in frowning silence. It occurred to Spain that Ed hadn't offered an opinion in regard to Vivian's brutal assault and seemed reluctant to do so now. Weighing this against what Lace Fayette had said about the old lawman, Spain thought, Ed doesn't want to get implicated. There were any number of reasons why a sheriff might choose to remain neutral in a deal like this. Ed might be afraid of Sid Vivian, as Lace had suggested; or he might be secretly favoring Lew Wade. One thing seemed certain: Kenyon didn't intend to take Sam's side of it.

The bounteous portion of beef and potatoes Gail had served him made Spain feel less irritable; the second cup of coffee warmed him so that he was lightly perspiring now. Observing how attentively Gail watched Sam, he felt sorry for her. It wasn't Gail's fault that her brother couldn't properly defend himself against Boxed W, or that a lady banker had talked a romantic fool into running errands for her.

Finally Kenyon said to Sam, "I guess you know Lin Graham died."

101

Spain saw Purdy wince at mention of the dead man. Sam, he supposed, couldn't abide the thought that he had killed a human being.

Gail moved over to Sam and put an arm around his shoulders; she said, "Lace Fayette told Clay she'd go your bail. She wants you to stay at the hotel until your trial is over."

Purdy thought about that, and Kenyon said soothingly, "Don't reckon the coroner's jury would object to that, just so you stay in town."

"But what'll happen here while I'm away?" Sam asked. "What's to keep Sid Vivian from running Sis off and burning the place down?"

"Lew Wade wouldn't stand for that," Kenyon said.

But Sam said stubbornly, "Sid Vivian does as he pleases. He told me no man could shoot a Boxed W rider and stay in Apache Basin — even if he shot in self-defense."

A deeper gravity rutted Kenyon's cheeks. "Sid had no right to tell you that," he said.

"He had no right to beat Sam unmercifully," Gail pointed out. "But he did."

Spain eased back from the table and fashioned a cigarette. He wondered if Vivian and Gillum had gone all the way into town with Bob. That uncertainty stirred a nagging sense of apprehension. Acting upon pure impulse, he stepped out to the stoop and stood there listening for a long moment. There was no sound, and presently he heard Sam Purdy say, "Vivian will burn this place down if I go to town."

Spain turned to the doorway and looked at Sam, seeing how unfit to fight he was; knowing how reluctantly he would ever fight. "What damned difference would it make?" he demanded.

Sam shrugged and glanced at Gail, as if ashamed to make this admission in front of her. "Maybe not much. But I'm not going to leave Sis here alone to face Sid Vivian's toughs."

"I don't see what choice you've got," Kenyon said. "You're under arrest, Sam, and you got to go with me."

The impact of those words altered Purdy's face; it tightened the frown on his chalky cheeks and compressed his bruised lips. "Suppose I refuse to go," he said flatly.

Kenyon wasn't prepared for that. He demanded, "You gone loco in the head?"

Purdy reached out and grasped one of the Winchesters Spain had tilted against the wall.

"No!" Gail cried. "You mustn't, Sam!"

103

But Purdy evaded her obstructing hands. Holding the Winchester unaimed but ready, he blurted, "I'm not leaving here, Ed. I just ain't!"

Ed Kenyon sat rigid, as if frozen to his chair. Shock and an overwhelming disbelief gave his voice an odd, high-pitched tone when he exclaimed, "You're loco! Pure loco!"

Spain had moved into the room so that he was a trifle behind and to the right of Kenyon. Now he stood looking at Sam, scarcely able to believe what he saw; when he glanced at Gail the expression in her startled eyes told him that she was equally astonished.

"Put down that gun!" Kenyon ordered. "Put it down, I say!"

Purdy shook his head.

Kenyon's right hand was within inches of his holster, yet he made no move to draw. He stared at Purdy as if seeing a total stranger; a dangerous, threatening stranger bearing no resemblance to the meek man he had known for years. Finally he turned and looked at Spain, his eyes keenly questing. "How about you, Clay? You siding him?"

Ignoring the question, Spain asked, "You sure about this, Sam? Real sure?"

Purdy nodded. "I've took all I'm going to take," he muttered, keeping his eyes on Kenyon. "I ain't leaving this place. Not alive."

"Why, you dim-witted damned fool!" Ed Kenyon shouted, indignant now and at the end of his patience. "Ain't it bad enough that you've killed a man, without making a damned outlaw play like this? Can't you see how a jury'll feel about it, and that there'll be no bail when you're caught?"

"I ain't leaving here, regardless," Sam said.

Gail asked urgently, "Won't you give him until tomorrow morning to decide, Sheriff Ed?"

"It's not up to him to decide!" Kenyon shouted, anger staining his age-mottled face. "By God, I'm the law, and I'm telling him to come with me now!"

As if punctuating that shouted explanation, a voice behind Spain announced, "He'll go with you, Ed."

It was Sid Vivian's voice.

And at that instant, as Spain loosed a whispered curse, Red Gillum's face and a pistol's snout appeared at the side window.

"Take the rifle away from him, Ed," Vivian said, and when that was accomplished, Sid stepped into the room and looked at Spain. "So you're the one," he mused, his voice surprisingly mild. "What you doing back here, Clay?"

Spain shrugged. Glancing at Gillum's covering gun, he understood how tightly the trap had been sprung, and how easy the springing had been, thanks to Kenyon's loud talking. This pair had walked right up to the house while Kenyon wagged his jaw.

As if guessing what was in his mind, Red called tauntingly, "Make a try, Spain. Go ahead and make one."

There was a moment, as Vivian came over to disarm him, when Spain thought there might be a chance. If any part of Sid's big body shielded him for an instant, he could make a play. But Vivian was wary as a stalking wolf; he came just near enough to lift the gun from the holster.

A huge relief showed in Ed Kenyon's face and in his voice when he said, "You boys showed up in the nick of time." Taking a pair of handcuffs from his hip pocket, he shackled Sam's wrists and muttered, "Now maybe you'll feel like you're arrested."

Red Gillum came into the kitchen, broadly smiling; he said to Sam, "So you went bronc on Sheriff Ed," and laughed in Purdy's face.

Spain glanced at Gail. Guessing how this must be for her, he marveled at her composure. Except for slim hands tightly clasped against her bosom, she revealed no sign of agitation. As Kenyon prodded Sam through the doorway, Gail said, "I'll bring your razor and some clean clothes tomorrow."

"Bring them to the jail," Kenyon said, a note of resentment still in his voice. "That's where he'll be."

Sid Vivian followed them out to the stoop, and now Gillum came over to Spain. Red didn't say anything, but his hot eyes told Spain how it was going to be when Kenyon rode off with his handcuffed prisoner.

Spain heard Ed ask, "What's this I hear about you ordering Purdy out of Apache Basin?"

"You heard right," Vivian replied. "He killed a Boxed W rider, didn't he?"

"That's a matter for the court to take care of," Kenyon said.

There was more to it, but their voices faded as they walked toward the corral. Presently, as Kenyon rode out of the yard with Purdy, he called back, "You keep your crew away from here, Sid. I don't want Miss Gail molested in any way."

When Vivian remained silent, Ed demanded, "You hear, Sid?"

"Sure," Vivian said impatiently. "What the hell you take me for?"

"Well, I just want it understood. You leave

this place alone."

Boxed W's big ramrod stood on the stoop until the diminishing sound of hoofs died out entirely. Gillum remained near Spain, gun in hand. When Vivian came into the kitchen, Red asked, "In here or outside?"

Vivian picked up the two Winchesters and toted them to the stoop; he jacked the loads from each weapon in turn and tossed them into the yard. Then he came in and picked up the lamp, transferring it from the table to a shelf behind the stove. When that was done he said, "In here."

"What are you going to do?" Gail demanded.

"We're going to teach Mr. Butinsky a lesson," Vivian said. He took out his pistol and stepped close to Spain and said, "Unbuckle your belt."

The arrogant command fanned the flames of Spain's resentment. He said rashly, "To hell with you," and, pitching forward, grasped Vivian's right arm with both hands, forcing the gun up. He tried desperately to swing Sid around so that his big body would protect him from Gillum's gun; but Vivian braced himself and commanded, "Tap him, Red!"

Gail's startled cry warned Spain. He ducked his head to one side so that the pistol's barrel struck a glancing blow above his right ear. But it was enough. He felt himself going down, and presently heard Vivian order, "Tie his hands."

Someone helped him up then, and he heard Vivian complain, "You didn't need to hit him that hard."

When Spain's eyes came into focus he understood that he was propped against a wall and that Red Gillum stood in front of him, as if waiting for something. Glancing past Red's freckle-blotched face, Spain saw Sid Vivian standing across the room in front of Gail, who was in a corner. He couldn't see Gail's face, but now he heard her ask, "Haven't you hurt him enough?"

Vivian ignored that. Looking at Spain, he asked, "You woke up, bucko?"

Spain shook his head, attempting to clear away the dizziness that gripped him. There was a throbbing ache all across the top of his head, and blood made a warm wetness on his right cheek.

"He's awake," Gillum said impatiently.

The redhead stood with both fists cocked and now Spain observed that the brown freckles on his knuckles matched those on his face.

"You hear what I'm saying?" Vivian demanded.

"To hell with you," Spain muttered, and tried to tug his hands free. But they were tightly belted behind him.

"You shot a Boxed W man," Vivian said. "You wounded Bob Teague. That means you're through in Apache Basin."

"And you slugged me, by God!" Gillum snarled.

Spain saw it coming. He tried to dodge away from those flashing fists, but they smashed against his face with an impact that knocked him hard against the log wall. Turning instinctively and lifting a shoulder to protect his face, Spain floundered away from the wall. Gillum knocked him into teetering retreat with successive rights and lefts to the face; he shouted gloatingly, "I'll teach you to slug me, you smart-alecky bastard!"

For what seemed an endless time, Spain had only a remote impression of what was happening to him. Fists thudded against his face and upper body. Knuckles raked his bandaged arm with a glancing blow, and the sharp pain forced a groan from him. Gillum loosed a pleased chuckle; he chortled, "Excuse me for hitting your gimpy arm," and deliberately targeted the wound again.

When Spain turned to protect it, Red

punished his face with deft, skin-peeling jabs. Not hard blows that might finish a man, but a slicing butchery meant to prolong this thing.

Spain went to his knees. He felt Gillum haul him up immediately. That didn't make sense, nor did Red's panting announcement: "Not yet, friend — not yet!"

Some time after that Spain heard Vivian call impatiently, "That's enough, Red. Finish him off."

Spain backed to the wall and stood propped against it. He didn't see the fist that knocked him down. There was a tremendous impact against his chest, repeated again and again. As if from a far distance he heard Gail cry, "You're killing him!"

After that there was a queer, empty silence while he slid into a pit of blackness. . . .

CHAPTER NINE

Fancy Anne remained seated while Jack Benteen came to the veranda. She said, "Take a chair, Handsome," and waited for him to sit down.

Faint lamplight from the shuttered front window gave her high-coiled hair a burnished copper shine; it complimented her full-lipped fleshy face and a bulging bosom that no fashionable gown could quite conceal. In the ten years that she had operated her establishment Fancy Anne had become an accepted part of Hondo's business life. Substantial citizens whose wives resented the Shiloh Alley parlor house pointed out that she treated her girls well, ran a quiet place, and, although dressing in the height of fashion, never invaded the respectable precincts of Residential Avenue.

"Hint of fall in the air tonight," Benteen said, taking a cigar from his vest pocket.

"Was it cool on Residential Avenue?"

Fancy Anne asked.

Benteen peered at her, not speaking as he dug out a match.

"Are you getting tired of the saloon business?" she asked casually.

"Why, no," Benteen said. He lit the cigar, his face quite sober in the match flare. He puffed on the cigar for a moment, then pitched it out to the street, muttering, "Must of broken it somehow."

"Somehow?" Fancy Anne taunted. "On Tipton's back porch?"

"What makes you say that?"

Fancy Anne made an open-palmed slapping gesture, two diamond rings setting up a glint of reflected lamplight. She said, "It's common gossip what you're up to, Jack. Both my girls have heard it."

"Talk," Benteen scoffed. "Just woman talk."

"It didn't start with women. It came from men. They think it's downright comical, after what Earl Tipton called my place."

"Well, it's just gossip, no matter who started it," Benteen insisted. "This is a gossipy town for a fact."

Fancy Anne moved her chair so that she faced him directly; she said, "If it's just gossip, then what were you doing in the alleyway behind Residential Avenue this

113

evening?"

"Who says I was there?" Benteen demanded.

"I do, Jack. When you went toward that part of town I tagged along, wanting to see whether you use the front door or the back door when you call on Eve Tipton."

Benteen was cornered, and knew it. Yet he made a desperate effort to wriggle out of a situation that held the threat of dire consequences. " 'Twas just a friendly visit," he said, forcing a bland and confident tone. "She's dabbling with water colors and had a picture she thought might look good in the saloon."

Fancy Anne laughed at him. She took a deep breath and then asked, "Does the Tipton woman use lilac perfume mixed into her paint?"

Benteen had no answer for that, and now she said derisively, "You smell like a pimp."

She had kept her voice low and calmly amiable, but now there was a plain note of anger in it as she announced, "I called on Earl Tipton at his office. I told that busybody what kind of a wife he has — a charity slut is what I called her!" She chuckled, adding, "You should've seen his face when I told him what was going on in his own house. And him calling my place a Gomorrah!"

"Did you tell him who it was?" Benteen asked.

Fancy Anne shook her head. "Maybe he can guess. Maybe he'll come looking for you with a gun. It would serve you right."

She gave him a little time to absorb that; she watched him rub his hands together and look at them as if he found them objects of absorbing interest. Finally she reached out and gripped his arm and asked, "Haven't I treated you good, Jack? Haven't I given you everything any woman could give a man?"

"Sure," Benteen agreed. "Sure you have."

"Then why'd you go tom-cattin' after that stylish slut? What did she ever do for you?"

Benteen remained silent, having no words to explain why a man might prefer a respectable woman to a parlor-house madam; why Eve's small, passionate body might be more desirable than this woman's full-blown voluptuousness.

Fancy Anne clung to his arm with possessive urgency; she said, "It must be the Irish in you, Jack. The Mick romance that makes you easy pickings for the flirty ones. Is that it, Jack?"

"Suppose," he said, subdued and repentant. "A man does foolish things some-times."

That pleased Fancy Anne, and so did the affectionate hug he gave her now. But she wanted a definite understanding, and so she asked, "Are you all through with her, Jack?"

When he didn't speak for a moment, she said bluntly, "Don't be forgetting that I hold a mortgage against the saloon."

A man turned in from the street. As he came to the veranda, Fancy Anne stepped to the doorway and called, "Company, girls!"

Presently, when the customer had gone inside, she came back to Benteen and asked, "Are you all through with Eve Tipton?"

"Yes," Benteen said gravely. "All through."

"Then let's go to the kitchen," Fancy Anne said happily, "and I'll fix you a cup of coffee to go with the birthday cake I made this afternoon."

"Birthday cake?" Benteen asked.

Fancy Anne laughed, wholly pleased. "You always forget your birthday, Jack. But I don't."

And then, as they went through the parlor, she said softly, "You're forty-five years old today. Old enough to have some sense."

Benteen thought, Too old to start over with another woman, and presently, looking at the white cake with its cluster of red candles, he said, "You're a great one, Anne. You are for a fact."

Clay Spain heard someone call his name; someone that seemed to be far away. When he opened his eyes the lamplight blinded him. He blinked his eyes, and as they came into focus he identified Gail Purdy's face.

"Can you raise up a trifle on your elbows?" she asked.

Spain nodded, and wondered why she had unbuttoned his shirt. The aromatic odor of liniment was quite strong, and now he became aware of a penetrating warmth along his right side. Yet the rest of his body felt cold.

Gail asked, "Can you get up a little, Clay?"

Spain moved, placing pressure on his elbows, and now, as pain stabbed his right side, he held himself rigid. In this moment all his senses cleared and he understood why he was on the floor of Sam Purdy's kitchen.

"I've got to bind your ribs," Gail said, her low voice calmly matter-of-fact. "Up just a trifle more, Clay."

Spain clamped his teeth against sharp splinters of pain. He got his back off the floor and held himself propped on his elbows while Gail swiftly maneuvered the shirt over his shoulders so that it was out of the way. Then she worked a four-ply fold of sheet around him, wrapping it tightly and fastening it with safety pins. When that was done she asked, "Can you sit up?"

Sweating now, Spain obeyed, and sat there while she drew the shirt up and buttoned it. "Did Red kick me?" he asked.

"Yes," Gail said. "Three times."

She went to the stove and came back with a cup of hot coffee. "Drink this."

Spain drank the coffee in three eager gulps, wanting its warmth against the cold knot of sickness in his stomach. "Thanks," he said, and handed her the empty cup. As she put it on the table he muttered, "So the redheaded bastard kicked me when I was down."

"It was awful," Gail said, and used her apron to wipe his perspiring forehead.

Some final fragment of shock ran out of him in a convulsive shudder, and now she said, "You should be in bed with plenty of blankets over you."

She waited a moment, watching him accept the necessity of getting up; then, knowing what had to be done, she got behind him and added her strength to the effort.

Except for one brief stab of pain, it wasn't

bad. He said, "The binding helps a lot."

But now he felt dizzy and nauseated. "I've got to step outside," he mumbled, and when she took his arm he shook her off, saying impatiently, "I'll be all right."

A man wanted to be alone at a time like this.

The retching was an agony that raked his side again and again. But at last it was over, and as he turned back to the stoop he was shivering. He said dully, "Weather's turning cold," and accepted Gail's supporting arm as she guided him to Sam's bedroom.

When he was stretched out on his back she said, "I'll take off your boots."

"Don't bother," Spain said. But he was too spent for resistance, and when she unbuckled his belt he made no protest. But presently, as Gail draped his pants over a chair, he muttered drowsily, "A hell of a thing."

Gail covered him with a blanket, then brought two quilts from her bedroom and put them over him also. She stood beside the bed for a moment, not sure in this dim light if his eyes were closed. When his breathing became deep and steady she went out to the kitchen and poured herself a cup of coffee.

The fire in the stove had died down and

the coffee was cold. That, somehow, seemed hugely depressing; a final straw. It demolished her last barrier of defense, so that now she gave in to a quiet, continued sobbing.

CHAPTER TEN

It was nearly noon when Spain awoke. His first sensation was of thirst. His mouth felt as dry as the sun-warped sole of a discarded shoe; when he licked his bruised lips they were cob-rough against his tongue.

Spain hunched up on an elbow, and grimaced at the multiple aches the motion brought. His chest, his shoulders, even the muscles of his face were quivering masses of misery. He was softly cursing when he noticed the glass of water on the commode beside his bed. Eagerly reaching for the glass, he grunted a final curse and drank it dry. He glanced toward the doorway then and saw Gail sitting at the kitchen window with a Winchester across her lap. Observing the down-tilted position of her head and the gentle rise and fall of her bosom, he understood that she was asleep.

The sight of her with a rifle — the futility of this girl standing guard, and of all that had led up to it — brought an overwhelming sense of depression to him. She might as well be sitting there with a feather duster in her hand for all the good it would do. One Winchester couldn't stop Boxed W, no matter who held it. Sid Vivian had proved that last night, and he would prove it again when he chose. Maybe might didn't make right, but it made sense. That was more than you could say for Gail Purdy sleeping with a gun in her lap, or for an interfering fool who'd got his ribs kicked in.

Spain threw back the blankets. He thought, I feel as if a shod bronc had stomped me, and he hated Red Gillum with a swift-rising fury that somehow sustained him as he got off the bed. Slowly, in the deliberate way of a man thinking out each successive move, Spain made it to the chair and picked up his trousers. His head was clear; too damned clear, for it registered the full degree of aching ribs and sore muscles as he pulled on his pants. This, by God, was what a man got for butting into a deal that didn't concern him. It was a fool's punishment for letting his itch for a woman get the best of him.

Damn Lace Fayette and her man-baiting body!

She had soft-talked him into the last fool

deal he'd ever get into. Let Cap Ledbetter and Jack Benteen and the rest of them run her errands for the privilege of gawking at her. And that's probably all they'd get out of it. Judging by the way she'd talked and acted, Dan Tennant probably hadn't got so much as a kiss. Wincing as he reached for his boots, Spain thought, She owes me more than that. A lot more.

It took him a long time to tug on his boots, and he was sweating when he eased into the kitchen. Gail had retrieved his pistol, holster, and rifle; they were on the table alongside a cup of cold coffee. He was at the stove, using his knife to make shavings for a fire, when Gail awoke. She peered at him through sleep-swollen eyes and said dully, "So you woke up." Then, as if abruptly aware of what was going on, she exclaimed, "You should be in bed!"

"I'm hungry," Spain muttered.

Gail took over the task of building a fire. She said, "You sit quiet while I fix breakfast."

Observing how efficiently she went about it, Spain watched her with a speculative interest. She wasn't one to hurry; working with an effortless ease, she placed a skillet over the crackling flames and then filled the coffepot from a water bucket beside the sink. Her cotton dress was wrinkled and her unbrushed hair a trifle frowzy. She was pale and drawn, and her cheekbones were more pronounced than usual. A bad night, Spain thought, and a bad evening before it. Yet even so, there was a self-sufficiency about her. Recalling how calmly she had accomplished the chore of binding his ribs, Spain mused, "You're quite a girl, Gail."

Presently, as they ate breakfast, Gail said, "I'd better go get Doc Randall to have a look at your ribs."

"No need for that," Spain said. The bacon and eggs made him feel better. He finished off his second cup of coffee and said, "Doc couldn't bind up my ribs any better than you did. Can't cook like you, either."

The praise puzzled Gail. She eyed him in contemplative silence, wondering at the abrupt change in him. It occurred to her now that she had liked this man without knowing exactly why. It wasn't his looks, for he couldn't be called handsome, unless a lean and shaggy tiger was handsome. But there was some quality that set him apart from other men, or a merging of qualities, so that he could be tough without being brutal, sensitive without being weak. He possessed a self-mocking humor that was an odd mixture of hardheaded fatalism and wistfulness. It was revealed in the crooked smile that slanted his bruised cheeks now; it was in the frank male interest of his bold eyes as he looked at her.

"Last night," she said, "you blamed me because you got into our trouble."

"Not your fault," he said. "My own — and Lace Fayette's. She talked me into coming here."

"So that's it," Gail mused.

"What do you mean — that's it?"

Gail shrugged and said thoughtfully, "I guess most of the men in Apache Basin are secretly in love with Lace Fayette."

"Not me," Spain said. "Secretly or otherwise."

That declaration didn't alter Gail's sober appraisal. She watched him fashion a cigarette and light it. Finally she asked, "Do you think they'll let Sam out on bail?"

Spain shook his head. "Not after the way he resisted arrest. Ed Kenyon won't forgive Sam for that." He chuckled, adding, "Ed was purely spooked — afraid of Sam and afraid of being afraid."

He got up and stepped gingerly over to the doorway and looked at his dead pony. Flies swarmed about the bay, and the sun was getting in its work. There was a horse in the corral, a shaggy, big-footed black with collar marks on his shoulders. "Is the black broke to saddle?" he asked.

"Yes. Why?"

"That dead horse is beginning to stink. He should be drug out of the yard."

"Well, you can't do it in the shape you're in."

"I could with a little help."

It took some doing. Gail stripped the saddle off the bay and put it on the black. She tried to talk Spain into letting her do the riding, but he refused, fearing she might get her slim fingers hurt in dallying the rope around the horn. But she did the ground-work, fastening the loop to the dead pony's hind foot.

Getting into the saddle was a painful chore for Spain, but finally he was astride the animal. Sitting quietly for a moment, he said, "Fetch my Winchester," and after she had brought it, he kept the rifle in his rein hand while making his dallies with the rope.

Slowly the black horse dragged the dead bay out to the flats beyond the barn. Keeping a wary eye on the surrounding country, Spain flipped his loop free and coiled the rope. When he got back to the yard Gail said:

"I'll unsaddle, Clay. You go lie down."

Spain followed that suggestion, and with

the Winchester beside him on the bed, he was soon asleep.

It was still daylight when he awoke. Gail stood in the doorway, saying, "Time to eat. Aren't you hungry?"

"Yes," Spain said. "Now that you mention it, I'm starving."

Gail smiled at him. "No wonder," she mused. "You've slept for almost eighteen hours."

"Eighteen hours!" Spain echoed, shaking his head. "You mean — this is tomorrow?"

Gail nodded. "At least, you went to sleep yesterday afternoon."

She had cooked a big pot of stew that tasted as good as it smelled, and there was a dried-apple pie for dessert. As always, the bounteous meal had its cheering effect on Spain, but afterward, as he sat in the kitchen while Gail washed the dishes, his sense of futility returned. "Boxed W is too big an outfit to buck," he said. "Even if Sam was a fighting man, which he isn't."

Gail went on with her dishwashing for a moment before asking, "Where would we go, Clay?"

"Anywhere, just so you get out of Apache Basin. Sid Vivian's got it in for Sam, and he won't let anything stop him."

Calmly, in the way of a woman repeating

an opinion she did not like but must agree with, Gail said, "Sam has tried running, and it did no good. We left Texas because of trouble with tough neighbors. I suggested we move to New Mexico. Sam got a nice little place started in Lincoln County, then sold out so he wouldn't get mixed up in the Murphy-Chisholm feud. Now his mind is made up. He says a man can't spend his whole life running away from trouble."

When Spain considered that in moody silence, Gail said quietly, "You left Mexico to get away from trouble. But you found trouble here. Perhaps Sam is right. Perhaps you can't run away from it, no matter where you go."

A remote rumor of hoofbeats stirred instinctive reactions, Gail wiping her hands on her apron and Spain reaching for his gun. She got to the doorway ahead of him; she said, "Someone in a buggy," and as Spain joined her she added, "Lace Fayette with Earl Tipton."

When the rig came into the yard, Spain looked at Lace and marveled at the swift awareness her presence brought, and resented it.

Lace gave him her frank attention; she asked, "Are you all right, Clay?" and when he nodded, she asked, "Whatever happened to your face?"

"Red Gillum got even," Spain said, observing that the long hot ride hadn't diminished the beauty of her face.

"Come have some coffee," Gail invited.

Tipton helped Lace down with the practiced gallantry of a knight assisting a queen. Watching this, Spain thought, He's got it too, and he wondered if that was why Tipton's wife had got herself gossiped about.

Tipton said to Gail, "Sam asked me to tell you that he's doing well. Nothing broken except his nose, which Dr. Randall has attended to quite satisfactorily."

"That beating was an outrageous thing!" Lace exclaimed. "Sid Vivian should be arrested for assault and battery. But Ed Kenyon won't do a thing. He's even threatening to arrest you for wounding Bob Teague."

"Is Teague hurt bad?" Spain asked.

"A bullet hole in his left thigh," Lace reported. She introduced Tipton, who shook hands with a grip that surprised Spain. She said, "Earl wants to get the whole story for his paper, which goes to press this evening."

Gail put the coffeepot on to heat while Tipton questioned Spain about the gun fight. The frail, scholarly newspaperman kept up a barrage of questions with polite

129

insistence on details, writing the answers in a notebook. Tipton seemed oblivious of Lace Fayette's presence now, but Spain wasn't. He couldn't keep his eyes off her. In all his years of footloose wandering he had never seen a woman so enticing, so fully resembling the image of a man's desire. As if sharing the magnetic attraction between them, Lace met his questing glance with a kindred appraisal; she asked, "Hadn't you better have Dr. Randall look you over, Clay?" When Spain shook his head, she asked, "What are your plans?"

"Well, I've got to move a herd of cattle to Tombstone or Benson," he said, "soon as I'm able to ride."

"How many men are with the herd?"

"Two."

She thought about that while Gail poured coffee into four cups. Finally she asked, "Couldn't the cattle be held here until you're fit to make the trip north?"

Spain shrugged, not much interested, but Tipton said with swift enthusiasm, "Say, that would solve your problem and Sam's too!"

"How come?" Spain asked.

It was characteristic of Tipton that he allowed Lace to explain. She said, "It would give you a chance to recuperate." Smiling at

Gail, she added, "And get some good home cooking while you're doing it."

"How would that benefit Sam?"

"Well, he's worried for fear Boxed W will burn this place while he's awaiting trial. I think Lew Wade would hesitate to try anything with three men here who know how to use guns."

It was, Spain thought, a logical proposition. The cattle could use a couple of week's rest. Jubal and Pratt could have their spree in town. Turning to Gail, he asked, "How does it sound to you?"

"Fine," she said without hesitation. "Just fine. I'm sure Sam would be in favor of it."

"How about water for the cattle?" Spain inquired.

"There's an old tank down on the flats. The pipe from the windmill has been disconnected, and the tank probably needs mucking out. But it wouldn't take much work to put it in operation."

Something caught at Gail's attention; she peered out the window and said, "Look, Clay — look who's coming into the yard."

Her voice was without excitement, but something in the odd flat tone of it warned Spain, so that he was already drawing his gun when he turned to see Sid Vivian and

Lew Wade ride through the gate, with Red Gillum and two other men behind them.

CHAPTER ELEVEN

Spain eased to the doorway, gun in hand. This, he supposed, was Lew Wade's method of imposing his will on Apache Basin's small ranchers; overwhelming them with a show of power. Wade lifted his right palm in a burlesque peace sign and called, "No need for a gun, Clay."

But the sight of Gillum's freckle-blotched face filled Spain with a rash and unreasoning belligerence so impelling that he aimed his pistol and shouted, "Get out of this yard, Gillum!"

"Hold on there!" Sid Vivian protested.

Spain ignored him. "Get out, Gillum, or I'll gut-shoot you!"

"Go on," Wade said nervously. "Do as he says."

Aware that Earl Tipton had stepped into the doorway beside him, Spain snapped impatiently, "Get back."

The splayed fingers of Red's right hand

were close to his holster, and his eyes were hot with an impulse to draw. He was at this moment as cocked and eager as a man could be.

"Stop that," Sid Vivian commanded.

Red spat tobacco juice and glanced at Vivian, who sat rigidly erect in the saddle. He said, "There's five of us, Sid."

But Vivian shook his head. "Ride out of the yard," he ordered harshly.

Gillum mumbled a curse, and as he rode toward the gate, Spain called, "Next time you get it, Red."

As if in a hurry to get this over with, Lew Wade said, "I stopped by to tell you that I've bought Jubal's and Pratt's shares of those Roman Six cows, and I'd like for you to get the remainder off my range."

"You bought them?" Spain asked.

"Two hundred and fifty head," Wade said. Smiling now, he added cheerfully, "I've got a bill of sale to prove my ownership."

Spain thought, This is Gus Jubal's way of getting even with me, and he was surprised that Jubal hadn't sold the entire herd. He asked, "You in the market for the rest of them?"

Before Wade could reply, Sid Vivian snapped, "No, we ain't. And you've got just twenty-four hours to get them Sonora scrubs off Boxed W range."

Keeping a wary watch on Sid and the other two riders, Spain inquired, "Who makes the decisions, Lew — you or Vivian?"

"I do, of course," Wade said. "But I accept Sid's advice on range conditions."

As if resenting that explanation, Vivian announced, "I'm giving you twenty-four hours to drive your cattle out of Apache Basin, Spain. If you're here after that, look out."

Earl Tipton came back into the doorway. "I'm a witness to that threat," he said excitedly, and peered at Lew Wade. "There's never been any legal proof that you approved of your foreman's highhanded doings. But now, unless you countermand the order he has just given, I have proof, and I shall publish it!"

Sid Vivian laughed at him. "You and your piddling newspaper," he jeered.

Lew Wade seemed more amused than annoyed. "Don't upset yourself over a saddle tramp who got run out of Mexico," he said soothingly.

But now, as Lace and Gail came out to stand beside Earl, Wade's face lost some of its blandness. His eyes revealed surprise, and something more; something that might have been old regret. Tipping his hat, he said, "I had no idea there were ladies

135

present."

"Are you going to countermand that order?" Tipton demanded.

While Wade hesitated, Lace Fayette inquired, "Do you still play *'Clair de Lune'* on the piano?"

"Yes," Wade said. "Occasionally." A reflective smile wreathed his smooth round face and he said, "It's exquisite. I'd like for you to hear it."

Wondering about this, Spain glanced at Lace, observing how intently she looked at Wade as she said, "Perhaps I shall, sometime." Then she asked, "Aren't you going to answer Earl's question?"

"What question?"

"About countermanding your foreman's order."

Wade turned to look at Vivian. He asked, "Don't you think we should give Spain a little more time, Sid?"

Vivian ignored that. He glanced at Lace Fayette and said angrily, "Why don't you stick to the banking business?" Then he wheeled his horse and rode out to join Red Gillum beyond the gate.

Wade shook his head. "Sid has no patience," he explained, as if apologizing for a child's tantrum.

"That's not all he doesn't have," Spain

said. And now, because this thing had rubbed his nerves raw, he shouted, "I'll move my cattle when it suits my convenience. And I'll shoot any man that interferes with me."

Then he went into the house and poured himself a cup of coffee.

Afterward, when the Boxed W riders were gone, Lace asked, "Will you bring your share of the herd here, Clay?"

Spain nodded. And thinking how tedious a chore it would be for one man, he loosed a chuckle of cynical amusement. After three years he was alone again, back where he had started. And afoot.

Earl Tipton came over to the table and reached for Spain's right hand and shook it with admiring energy. "That," he announced, "was the most courageous thing, the way you made Red Gillum leave the yard. It was magnificent. The odds were five to one against you."

"No," Spain said. "Four to one. Lew Wade doesn't wear a gun." Aware of Lace Fayette's continuing regard, he asked mockingly, "Have you got me figured out?"

She nodded. "I think so, Clay." Some secret emotion warmed her eyes so that they were shining as she said softly, "I think you're the bravest man I've ever known."

That embarrassed Spain. All three of them were looking at him, and Earl exclaimed, "I subscribe to that opinion!"

It occurred to Spain that Gail had not spoken to him since the Boxed W group had come into the yard. She didn't now. To look at her you'd think nothing unusual had happened here. He asked, "Why so quiet, Gail?"

She shrugged and went to the stove. "Anyone want more coffee?"

"Not me," Lace said.

And Earl Tipton suggested, "We'd better be going. I've got to get out a paper this evening."

At the doorway Lace asked, "Hadn't you better ride in with us and let Dr. Randall look you over, Clay?"

"Don't need him," Spain said. Strongly aware of her continuing regard, he added, "But I'm going to need a horse. And a rider or two." He looked at Gail. "Mind if your star boarder spends the night in town?"

"Of course not," she said.

"You mean you won't miss me at all?" Spain demanded with mock concern.

"I mean you're free to come and go as you please," Gail said, her voice quite sober.

When Spain's saddle and Winchester had been stowed in the back of the buggy, he climbed up beside Lace and gave Gail a farewell salute. Seeing how gravely she watched his departure, he called, "Anything you want in town?"

Gail shook her head. She stood there on the stoop and watched until the buggy was far out on the flats. Then she went to the barn and did the chores.

Joe Pratt stood at the Shamrock bar with Gus Jubal and described the girl he had visited in Fancy Anne's parlor house. "She's just my height and about my weight, and the prettiest blonde gal you ever set eyes on."

Jubal kept peering into the back-bar mirror, watching the doorway's reflected batwings. He said, "No telling when Clay Spain will hit town. We better be leaving, Joe."

But Pratt was half drunk and wholly pleased with Hondo. "Her name is Lilybelle," he said. "Now, there's a name that's something special. And so is she. When a girl looks pretty in the daytime, she's really pretty."

"Horse apples," Jubal muttered disgustedly. "A Yaqui squaw with a harelip and no teeth would look good to you."

Joe shook his head. "I got an eye for beauty," he insisted. Placing a double eagle on the bar, he ordered a new round, and chuckled as the night bartender poured the drinks. "I always heard Hondo was a nice town, but I didn't know it was this nice."

"Nice, hell," Jubal scoffed. "One little old spraddle house, and not a roulette wheel in town. That's what I want — roulette. You can't make no money in a spraddle house. All you can do is spend it. But a man might get lucky and clean up a big bundle in one of them Tombstone gamblin' halls. He might make a fortune in one night."

"I've heard tell," Joe agreed. "Must be quite a town, Tombstone."

"Best in the west," Jubal bragged. "And if it's sprawly women you want, why, they got more'n a man could cover in a month's time."

"Not like Lilybelle," Pratt said. "She's something special, Gus." He grinned sheepishly, adding, "Makes me feel bigger'n Billy-be-damn just to look at her. Like I'm the main stud."

"You won't feel so big if Clay Spain comes busting in here," Jubal warned, watching the batwings. "I say we pull out right now."

Pratt shook his head. "I promised Lilybelle I'd call on her tonight."

Jubal cursed. "You want to face Clay Spain? You want to get yourself shot?"

"Clay won't like what we done," Joe admitted, "but he's got no call to shoot us. We just sold our rightful share, is all."

Jubal laughed at him. "Spain'll be mad enough to cut out our hearts and eat 'em." He turned toward the doorway. "To hell with you, Joe. I'm leaving right now."

At the batwings he called, "Come on. Don't be a fool."

"I promised Lilybelle I'd see her tonight," Pratt said. "I got to keep my word."

Presently, as Joe watched the bartender light the bracket lamps, he asked, "Do you know Lilybelle?"

"Who doesn't?" the barkeep muttered. "She's a whore, ain't she?"

Joe didn't like that. He said solemnly, "Don't seem right to call her one, she's so pleasant and nice-acting."

The bartender spat into a cuspidor. "They all smile and honeyfuss for a man who's got a pocketful of money."

"Well, you got to admit she's pretty," Joe said.

"You seen Lace Fayette?"

Joe shook his head.

"Well, compared to her, your Lilybelle looks like a wore-out sock on a trash heap."

"That ain't so!" Joe shouted. "By grab, I've saw some pretty gals in my time, and I say she's a beaut!"

He finished his drink and was having another when Cap Ledbetter stopped at the batwings, saying, "Man at the barn wants to see Joe Pratt."

"Thanks," Joe said. "Come have a drink with me."

"Mighty kind of you to offer it," Cap said, "but I'm on my way to supper."

When Cap went on up the alley, Joe said, "This is a nice town, for sure. Nice people in it."

He gulped down his drink, picked up his change, and went outside.

A lantern hung in the livery's wide doorway, where Jubal was saddling his horse. Gus probably wanted to make one more try at getting him to leave town, Joe thought. But he wasn't leaving. Not tonight. Not with a girl like Lilybelle waiting to entertain him. A man didn't get to know a girl like that every day. He glanced at the parlorhouse veranda, hoping to see Lilybelle sitting there. But the lamplit veranda was deserted. What a girl she was! It did a man good just to look at her. Joe smiled, remembering how her long blonde hair had looked fluffed out on the pillow.

Joe staggered as he crossed the alley. He grinned and said, "Must be a trifle tipsy."

Jubal's horse was in the doorway, all saddled. But Gus had disappeared. Joe glanced into the harness room. "Where you at, Gus?"

"Back here," Jubal called, "doin' my duty." He grunted and said, "Something I want to tell you about Clay Spain."

Pratt walked unsteadily along the runway between twin rows of stalls. It was dark here, and he asked, "Which stall you in?"

"Here," Gus said.

Then something exploded against Joe's head.

CHAPTER TWELVE

Clay Spain was alone in the buggy when he drove into Shiloh Alley at dusk. Tipton, eager to get the afternoon's big story into type, had accepted his offer to put up the rig. And Lace had got out at the hotel, saying, "I'll meet you in the dining room, Clay."

Recalling her expressed intention of obtaining riders for his roundup, Spain thought, She'll find out different. Getting men to gather cows on Boxed W range wouldn't be easy, even for Lace Fayette. Not after what had happened to Sam Purdy.

Spain was within a dozen yards of the livery when Gus Jubal rode out of the lantern-lit doorway and turned northward. "Where you going?" Spain called sharply.

Jubal wheeled his horse. "Clay?"

"Yes," Spain said. Warned by a glint of reflected lamplight on metal, he drew and fired as Jubal's gun exploded.

Spain heard a window break somewhere

behind him. He saw Jubal tilt sideways, and now Gus yelled, "I quit!"

Jubal gigged his nervous horse into the doorway's shaft of lamplight. His right arm hung straight down and his gun was gone. "I'm shot in the shoulder," he whimpered.

The night bartender came out of the Shamrock. Fancy Anne and her two girls stood in the parlor-house doorway as Cap Ledbetter ran up and panted, "What's going on?"

Spain watched Jubal dismount with the deliberate slowness of a man in pain. He asked, "Did you sell Wade my mules and the camp outfit?"

"No," Jubal said, and held a palm tight pressed against his bloodstained shirt. "They're here, in the corral."

Spain got out of the rig. He said, "I warned you not to draw against me. Where's Joe?"

Jubal ignored the question. "I need a doctor," he muttered, and walked up the alley.

The shots had attracted the town's attention. Men came from all directions, asking questions. Earl Tipton hurried up to Spain and asked breathlessly, "What happened?"

"An ex-partner took a shot at me," Spain said, and now, as Sheriff Kenyon arrived, he added, "He broke somebody's window."

"What's his name?"

"Gus Jubal."

"Did he shoot first?"

Spain nodded, and now Kenyon asked, "Why did he shoot at you?"

"Why don't you ask him?"

"Maybe I will," the old lawman said, a rising irritability sharpening his voice. "And maybe I'll be asking you some questions later on. It strikes me that you've got a habit of getting into trouble."

Spain grinned at him. Sheriff Ed's long-standing rule against gun fights had been blasted wide open during the past couple of days. "This is a troublesome country," Spain said, and he was elbowing his way through a crowd of bystanders when Lace Fayette asked:

"Are you all right, Clay?"

"Sure," he said, pleased by her concern. Taking her arm, he escorted her along the dark alley. "Were you worried about me?"

Her arm tightened so that his knuckles were pressed against her side. "Yes," she murmured. "I thought you'd been shot from ambush."

Spain chuckled. "Nice to have someone interested. Makes a man feel good to know somebody cares whether he gets shot or not." Then, impelled by an urge he couldn't put down, Spain said, "Wait a minute."

He got his good arm around her; he brought her against him with an abruptness that hurt his injured ribs. "Been wanting to do this," he said.

And then he kissed her.

For a moment she was a soft, cushioned shape within the tight circle of his arm, receptive to his demanding lips. Then her hands put an increasing pressure against him and she protested, "Someone coming, Clay."

Spain swore softly. As he took her arm, the oncoming man asked, "Somebody get shot?"

"Wounded is all," Spain said. Escorting Lace across Main Street, he asked resentfully, "Why did he have to come along just then?"

Lace smiled at him. "Perhaps because you're more bold than a man should be on such short acquaintance."

Spain chuckled, wholly pleased with himself and with her. He thought, Evening is young yet. The kiss had roused a demanding need in him. Escorting her into the hotel dining room, he basked in a warming glow of anticipation. Here was a woman to make a man hungry in more ways than one.

The meal was thoroughly enjoyable. Lace

seemed oblivious of the attention they attracted from other tables; discussing the irrigation project, she asked, "Don't you think it's a marvelous idea?"

Frankly contemplating the beauty of her lamplit face, Spain mused, "Marvelous is right."

"I mean the irrigation project," Lace said reprovingly.

Spain grinned. "I'll take your word for it," he said. Recalling her brief conversation with Lew Wade that afternoon, he asked, "Is Wade a musician?"

"He plays the piano surprisingly well. Seems to have a deep feeling for music."

"Didn't know he had a piano."

"Wade got one about a year ago," Lace said. "Had it freighted in from San Francisco. He's an odd man, Clay. I don't understand him. No one does."

Thinking back, Spain said, "He always acted like a man smart enough to have his foreman do the dirty work."

"Perhaps," Lace admitted. "But I believe there's more to it than that. Sometimes I have the feeling that Lew is afraid of Sid Vivian — that he's more afraid than the poorest nester in Apache Basin."

That idea seemed absurd to Spain. "What's he got to be afraid of? It's his ranch, isn't it?"

"I know it seems ridiculous," Lace admitted. "But Lew Wade doesn't act the way a normal person should."

Spain grinned at her. "He's normal enough to have a case on you, isn't he?"

Lace nodded. "But still his foreman and crew are trying to scare homesteaders out of joining the water association that I'm backing."

Spain considered that angle, and found no answer to it. He said, "Lew acts a trifle foolish at times, but I think he's foolish like a fox. I think it's to keep people like Ed Kenyon pacified. Whenever the Boxed W crew does something rough, Lew puts on his Gentle Annie act so folks won't think he's to blame."

"Perhaps," Lace said, "but I don't think that's it." Examining the little watch pinned to her blouse, she exclaimed, "Almost eight o'clock!"

"So?"

"I promised Earl I'd help him with the paper this evening. I've got to go now, Clay."

Hugely disappointed, Spain asked, "How long will it take?"

"All evening, I'm afraid. And I've got to find at least two men for your roundup."

"Waste of time," Spain predicted, and

now, paying for their dinner, he asked, "Can't Tipton get along without your help?"

Lace laughed at him, chiding, "Don't be a bad influence, Clay." Going on to the door, she said, "Thanks for an enjoyable supper."

Spain shrugged, and, understanding that a night's sleep in a hotel bed was all that remained for him, rented a room. Going up the stairs, he thought, Damn Tipton and his newspaper. He had his shirt off when Ed Kenyon knocked on the door.

Accepting the one rickety chair, Ed asked, "Why did you hit Joe Pratt?"

"Hit him?" Spain demanded. "Hell, I haven't seen him for three days. Who says I hit him?"

"He was a partner of yours, same as Jubal," Kenyon said. "And he sold his share of Roman Six cows to Lew Wade."

"Sure, sure," Spain agreed. "But that doesn't mean I hit him. What happened to Pratt?"

"Well, Cap Ledbetter found him spraddled out cold in a stall with a bloody crease across his skull. When Pratt came to he said somebody knocked him down. But he won't say who it was."

Spain thought instantly, Jubal! He asked, "How much cash did Joe have left?"

"Nine dollars and sixty cents."

Sure now that his hunch was right, Spain said, "Gus Jubal knocked Joe down and robbed him. You'll find plenty of cash on Gus."

Kenyon frowned. "No way to prove it. Jubal left on the stage to Tombstone." The old lawman seemed weighted by the gravity of his thinking. "No bad trouble for ten years. Then three men get shot in three days. By God, it's awful."

"You sure Jubal took the stage?" Spain asked.

Kenyon nodded. Presently he asked, "When you leaving, Clay?"

"Soon as I get my cattle gathered."

"Well, I hope it's soon," Kenyon said, and went to the door. "You stir up too much trouble."

It was late when Earl Tipton closed his office and went home, carrying a copy of the *Hondo Herald*. There was a light in the parlor. When he came onto the veranda he saw Eve sitting in the shadows, her blonde hair down around her shoulders.

"Thought you'd be in bed," he said.

"I was. But I couldn't sleep."

Earl opened the newspaper, holding it so that window lamplight revealed the front-page headlines. He said, "Best issue I've ever published. I'm really proud of it."

Eve read the headlines: "Man Shot in Shiloh Alley." "Lin Graham Dies." "Clay Spain Bucks Boxed W."

"Who is Spain?" she asked.

"The bravest man I've ever met," Earl said. "He stood up to Boxed W when they had him outnumbered five to one. And he shot it out with a tough character named Gus Jubal."

"My goodness," Eve mused. "He must be something."

A headline farther down the page caught her attention: "Malicious Gossip." Leaning forward, she read the short item aloud: "A well-known woman called at this office and made a slanderous statement about a lady who lives on Residential Avenue — a statement so vile that no right-thinking person would believe it. Needless to point out, the purveyor of gossip was retaliating for an editorial that was recently printed in these columns."

Eve glanced at her husband. His face revealed neither anger nor interest. She asked, "Why did you print this, Earl?"

"Well, to show her I wouldn't be intimidated, for one thing. And to prove how ridiculous the gossip was. Such rumors should be brought out into the open, where the white light of truth can expose them for what they are."

Eve shivered. She drew her kimono tighter about her shoulders. "Who was the gossip about?"

"You," Earl said, folding the newspaper.

"Me?"

Earl nodded. "Fancy Anne is a thoroughly unprincipled creature who'll say anything for spite."

"Spite?"

"Because I called her place a Gomorrah."

"But are you sure she meant me?" Eve demanded.

Earl smiled and patted her arm. "Yes, dear. That's what makes it so vile. So ridiculous."

"Did she say who the man was supposed to be?"

Earl shook his head. "How could she?" Then he said, "I'll be out of town for a day or two. Perhaps three."

Eve didn't seem to hear him, for she said, "It's odd that Fancy Anne didn't name the man."

"Who would she name?" Earl said impatiently. "Did you hear me say I'm going to be away for a few days?"

Eve nodded.

"You'd never guess what I'm going to do,"

he went on.

"Call on the editor of the *Tombstone Epitaph*?"

Earl shook his head.

"A meeting of editors in Tucson?"

"No," he said, enjoying this.

"Then what?"

"I'm going on a roundup. I'm going to help Clay Spain gather his cattle at Cartridge Creek and bring them to Sam Purdy's place."

"Why?"

"As a favor."

"But why should you do such a thing?"

"Well, the poor man has some cracked ribs and an injured arm. But he stood up to Boxed W, and I'm all for him. Lace Fayette has secured the loan of horses from Cap Ledbetter."

"Who else is going to help Spain?"

"The saloonkeeper in Shiloh Alley."

"You mean — Jack Benteen?" Eve demanded.

When Earl nodded, she exclaimed, "Oh, no! Not you — and Jack Benteen!"

"Why not?" Earl asked, baffled.

But Eve was past answering; she lay back in the chair, letting hysterical laughter have its way with her.

"What's so funny about that?" Earl demanded.

Eve tried to talk, and couldn't. She laughed until tears came, until she was breathless and spent. Then, wiping her wet cheeks with a kimono sleeve, she said, "I'm sorry, Earl. But it seems so comical. A newspaper publisher and a saloonkeeper, of all people."

"I still don't see why it's comical," he muttered.

"Oh, but it is," Eve insisted, laughing again. "It really is."

Earl smiled, accepting her word for it. There were many things about Eve he didn't understand. This odd sense of humor, he supposed, was just another facet of her complex femininity. He said, "It's getting cool out here. Let's go in and have some hot cocoa. It will help you sleep."

CHAPTER THIRTEEN

"Meet my wife," Earl Tipton said.

This was in the doorway of Ledbetter's Livery soon after sunup, with two mules already packed and three horses saddled.

Spain tipped his hat and took the hand Eve Tipton offered. She wore a black silk shawl against the morning coolness. Her blue eyes, set wide in a heart-shaped face, were frankly appraising as she smiled and said, "I've heard about you."

Spain thought, I've heard about you, too. Surprised that she should have come here, he watched as Tipton introduced Benteen, and saw color briefly stain her cheeks. She didn't offer her hand to the saloonkeeper. He said, "Glad to meet you, ma'am," and then gave his attention to tightening a cinch.

Understanding how it was between them, Spain felt sorry for Earl Tipton. But the newspaperman seemed proud to have his wife here; he buckled on a pair of borrowed chaps and asked her, "Do I look like a cowboy now, Eve?"

Eve smiled and nodded. As Earl climbed into the saddle she said to Spain, "Please watch out for him. He hasn't been on a horse in years."

Presently, riding out of town with his two-man crew, Spain said amusedly, "This is the oddest outfit ever went on a beef gather."

Jack Benteen gave him a slyly speculative regard; he grinned and said, "Damned if it isn't."

They both chuckled, but Earl saw nothing odd about it. "I did considerable horseback riding in the East," he announced. "And Mr. Benteen worked as a cowboy in his youth."

"Call me Jack," Benteen said. "That 'Mister' stuff makes me feel six years older'n God."

Presently, as if voicing a thought that nagged him, the saloonkeeper said, "Nobody but Lace Fayette could've talked me into a deal like this."

They were crossing the southern slope of the Horseshoe Hills when Spain saw a rider approaching; soon after that he identified Gail Purdy on the big-footed black, and guessed she was going in to visit Sam.

When Gail came up to them she glanced

at the pack mules and asked, "Roundup?"

Spain nodded, amused by her obvious surprise that Tipton and Benteen were going on a gather. Observing how well dressed she was, with a ruffled white blouse, pleated skirt, and polished black boots, he said, "So Hondo gets a treat today."

"How are your ribs?" she asked, not smiling.

"A trifle achy, but not bad."

"You shouldn't be riding," Gail said, and using her heels on the black, she rode off.

"There's a fine young woman," Tipton reflected. "She has the fortitude of a pioneer."

"And not bad-looking," Benteen said, smiling.

They were, Spain thought, as different as two men could be, yet they were involved with the same woman. And both were influenced by Lace Fayette. Recalling the brief embrace in Shiloh Alley last night, he realized now that Lace had accepted his kiss without responding to it; that even though she had been concerned about his welfare, she hadn't shared the thrusting eagerness her lips had aroused in him. It seemed odd. . . .

"You think we can gather your cattle in a couple of days?" Benteen asked.

Spain nodded. "Three days at most."

Thinking of the chore ahead, he wondered how badly the Roman Six cattle were scattered. Sid Vivian, he supposed, had chosen the best of the herd. The remaining cows might be scattered from hell to breakfast.

They evidently were, for he glimpsed only ten Roman Six brands during the ride to Cartridge Creek. It was sundown when they unpacked the mules and built a supper fire. Afterward, sitting around the glowing coals, Spain altered his prediction. "We'll be lucky to gather fifty head tomorrow," he said.

"Maybe Lew Wade will send some men over to help us," Benteen suggested cynically. Then he added, "Sid Vivian isn't going to like me much after this. He'll probably take his trade to Soos Mendoza's place."

Earl Tipton reached over and patted Benteen's shoulder. He said, "A man has to do what he thinks right, regardless of the cost. I'm proud of you, Jack, and proud to be with you."

Watching the saloonkeeper's firelit face, Spain saw embarrassment alter it as Benteen said, "I just let Lace Fayette talk me into this, is all."

Later, when Tipton and Benteen were in their blankets, Spain walked out into the brush with his Winchester and spent upwards of an hour listening for sounds of travel. It didn't seem logical that Sid Vivian would start anything the first night — he'd be more likely to wait until the gather had been made — but there was no telling what a man like Sid would do.

When Spain came back into camp the fire had died down to one cherry-red ember. Benteen was snoring, but Tipton asked, "Any sign of trouble, Clay?"

"Not a sign," Spain said. Bending over hurt his ribs, and he asked, "How about giving me a hand with these boots?"

"Gladly," Earl agreed. When he had tugged the boots off, he asked, "How early do you want breakfast in the morning?"

"So we can be riding by first daylight."

"I'm a light sleeper," Earl said, "and a fairly good cook. I'll get breakfast."

Remembering that Cap Ledbetter had called this scholarly newspaperman a Yankee dude, Spain said, "You're all right, Earl. You are for a fact."

They were asaddle at daylight, with Benteen grouchy despite three cups of Earl's coffee. "Didn't sleep worth a damn," the saloonman complained.

"But you did," Tipton insisted. "You slept like a log."

"How the hell would you know?" Benteen demanded sourly.

"Because I didn't sleep — worth a damn," Earl admitted.

They gathered thirty-four cows that day after riding long, brush-popping circles that brought saddle blisters to Benteen and Tipton. "Can't understand it," Spain said at the supper fire that evening.

The second day, with Earl loose-herding the little gather, Spain and Benteen brought in only twenty-one head between them. "At this rate it'll take until Christmas," Benteen complained. "I got a business to take care of in town."

"Then go take care of it," Spain said.

But after supper Benteen felt better. "Maybe we'll run into a big bunch tomorrow," he said.

The third day was worse. Spain didn't find a Roman Six cow all morning. By noon he was fifteen miles from camp, working the roughs south of Lew Wade's ranch headquarters, when he saw something that astonished him: a grown cow wearing a freshly burned Boxed W.

For a moment, as he peered at the brand, Spain couldn't understand it. Why would Boxed W be branding grown stock? Then, with the answer forming in his mind, Spain dismounted and broke off a mesquite branch. Using it for a long pencil, he drew a Roman six in the dust, then transformed it into a *W* by the simple process of changing the *VI* to *W* with one slanting line and adding lines about it to complete the box.

Spain understood then why each day's gather had decreased. Lew Wade had bought only half the herd, but his crew had taken more than that. Much more. Judging by the little bunch being held at Cartridge Creek, the Boxed W crew had picked up over four hundred cows.

Looking at the brindle cow, Spain muttered, "You've got a calf hidden around here." He rode up a rocky bench and sat there, watching the cow. He wanted her and the calf for evidence; he wanted Ed Kenyon to see that fresh-worked brand. It seemed fantastic that so big an outfit would steal cattle. Altering brands was done by the little fellows, the homesteaders and greasy-sack outfits that stole from the big boys. Why should Lew Wade, who owned most of the cattle in Apache Basin, go in for such thievery?

Keeping a watch on the brindle cow, Spain sought an explanation, and found it. This whole deal was a spite proposition. Spite had impelled Gus Jubal to sell half the herd, and Sid Vivian had vented his spite by taking most of the remaining cattle. Recalling the talk at Purdy's place — how forcibly Vivian had refused to buy the other half of the cows — Spain thought, Wade may not know about the worked-over brands. More likely it was Sid Vivian's doing.

"Vivian and Gillum," Spain muttered, hating them both.

There were two bastards that needed trimming down to size. Just thinking about what they had done to him and to Sam Purdy whipped up a blazing resentment in him.

When the brindle cow walked slowly northward, Spain watched until she joined her calf in a mesquite thicket. Easing along the ridge to get behind them, he caught a glimpse of Boxed W headquarters directly north of him. Surprised that he was so near, Spain focused his eyes on the dusty yard with its array of corrals, sheds, blacksmith shop, and bunkhouse loosely surrounding the main building. There was no sign of activity in the yard, but he observed a considerable haze of dust some five or six miles west of the ranch. Range branding, he guessed, and wondered if Lew Wade knew what was going on.

Spain gave the yard another appraisal. He

said, "One way to find out," and rode down the north slope of the ridge.

Boxed W headquarters seemed unchanged, its treeless yard aglare in noon sunlight. A few horses dozed in one of the pole corrals and flies swarmed about a huge trash heap beyond the kitchen stoop. Observing the countless tin cans there, Spain wondered if the same ancient Chinaman did the cooking. The blacksmith shop was deserted, but Spain wasn't sure about the bunkhouse. Nudging his gun loose in the holster, he kept an eye on the open doorway as he quartered across the yard.

The tinkling music of a piano came to him as he pulled up before the front gallery. It seemed odd to hear music in this place. He wondered what the crew thought about Lew Wade's hobby. He could guess Vivian's reaction; big Sid probably referred to it as hogwash.

Keeping a wary watch on the yard, Spain dismounted and stepped onto the gallery. Here he paused and peered westward. Detecting no sign of approaching riders, he opened the screen door and went inside. The parlor was as he remembered it, a spacious room with well-filled bookshelves flanking a huge fireplace on the south wall. Only the piano and the plump-faced man that played it seemed different. Unaware of his presence, Wade fingered the keys in the trancelike fashion of a concert pianist. Tousle-haired and needing a shave, he looked ten years older than the bland, neatly garbed man that had ridden into Purdy's yard three days ago.

"You make nice music," Spain said.

Wade stopped playing instantly. He peered at Spain astonished, yet some inherent graciousness controlled that astonishment so that his voice was calmly polite as he said, "Have a chair, Clay."

"I came to ask one question," Spain announced, "and then I'm leaving."

"One question? About what?"

"About a full-grown brindle cow that's carrying a fresh Boxed W brand."

Expecting to see surprise or consternation or disbelief, Spain was baffled by the benign smile Wade gave him as he said, "Why, that's easily explained."

"I mean a Roman Six brand that's been worked into a Boxed W."

Quite unconcerned, Wade picked up a pencil and made notations on a sheet of paper clipped to the music rack. "I'm composing a song," he explained. "Want to get these notes written down before I forget them." Then, putting away the pencil, he said, "I call it 'Moonlight Lace.' It was inspired by Lace Fayette. I think she's —"

While he sought a word to describe her, Spain suggested, "Exquisite?"

"Yes, yes. That's precisely what she is. The most exquisite woman I've ever known." Wade sighed, adding, "But she doesn't seem to share my feeling at all."

"Maybe she'd like you better if you quit bucking her irrigation scheme," Spain said.

That seemed to irritate Wade. "What right have people to spread such gossip?" he exclaimed. "Naturally I'm not in favor of losing water that my cattle need, but I'm not fighting the water association. How could I, when it's only in the process of being formed?"

Spain grinned at him. "There are ways," he said. "Sid Vivian seems to know them."

"Sid Vivian! To hear the talk that's going around, you'd think he was a master criminal!"

"Maybe he is, and you're the only one that doesn't realize it," Spain said. "Do you know your crew is altering Roman Six brands?"

Wade nodded.

"And you permit it?"

"Why shouldn't I?" Wade asked, seeming surprised at the question. "It's simpler to do that than to vent the Roman Six and then burn a Boxed W."

Spain peered at him, not sure whether this man was putting on a deliberate performance or actually believed what he was saying. It seemed impossible that Lew Wade could be so gullible — that the owner of a big outfit would be so easily tricked by a spiteful foreman.

Still undecided, Spain asked, "Do you know how many brands were altered?"

"About a hundred and fifty, as of yesterday," Wade said. "The crew is still branding, over at West Tank."

Spain laughed at him. "They've probably altered three hundred, and they're still at it."

"But I only bought two hundred and fifty head."

"That's the point."

"I don't understand."

Convinced now that he didn't, Spain said, "I've worked that country along the south bend of Cartridge Creek for three days with two riders. So far we've collected fifty-six head. I rode all morning and found only one cow, a Roman Six that had been turned into a Boxed W."

Wade still didn't seem to understand. He asked, "What does that indicate, except that your cows have scattered quite a bit? That's natural after the herd was cut by my crew."

"It indicates just one thing. You bought two hundred and fifty head but you're branding better than four hundred."

"No," Wade protested. "That's not right."

"Not right," Spain agreed, "but it's so."

"I can't believe it," Wade said, shaking his head. "Why should Sid brand more cattle than I bought?"

"Because he hates my guts. He and Gillum."

Wade thought about that for a moment. When he spoke he seemed less confident. "I suppose Sid dislikes you for interfering in the Purdy affair," he admitted. "Sid is used to having his own way. He's a trifle rough at times, but it takes a rough man to run a big ranch."

"Not that rough," Spain said. "And not that crooked."

"Sid isn't crooked. He's no thief. No one ever accused him of that. Not even his worst enemies."

"I do," Spain said. "I say your foreman is a goddamn thief, and I intend to prove it." Turning to the doorway now, Spain added, "I'm going to get two hundred and fifty head of cattle off this range, regardless of what brand they're wearing."

That threat startled Lew Wade. He held up a soft white palm. "No, Clay. Don't start a thing like that. It would mean shooting."

"Sure," Spain agreed. At the doorway he asked, "You want to head it off while there's still time?"

"How?"

"By ordering Sid Vivian to deliver two hundred cows at my camp during the next twenty-four hours."

Wade shook his head. "I couldn't ask him to do that," he said in a low, regretful voice. "Sid would never agree to it."

"Ask him, hell," Spain muttered. "Just tell him to do it. And what difference does it make whether Sid agrees or not?"

Wade shrugged. Some furtive thought caused his eyes to shift, and resignation was a plain thing in his voice when he said, "I own this ranch, but Sid runs it. There's — well, we have an understanding to that effect."

"So?" Spain said, and recalling Lace Fayette's opinion that this man was afraid of his foreman, he thought, She's right, by God! It seemed fantastic. Even now, with the proof before him, Spain could scarcely believe it.

Why should Lew Wade be afraid of his own ramrod?

And how had Sid Vivian instilled fear into the man who paid his wages?

Shrugging off the riddle of that, Spain said quietly, "I'm sorry for you, Lew." From the doorway, he added, "It may take some doing, but I'm going to get those cattle."

CHAPTER FOURTEEN

Shortly after noon Earl Tipton glimpsed three riders coming toward the holding ground where he loose-herded the Roman Six gather. He could not identify them at that distance, but he thought at once, Boxed W men, and was wholly apprehensive.

Where, he wondered, were Spain and Benteen? They should have made their morning circles and brought in some cows by this time. Earl scanned the brush, hoping to see the dust that signaled driven cows, and saw none.

Nervous now, he rubbed a beard-stubbled jaw and wondered what he could do if the three men decided to scatter these cows that had been gathered with such tedious toil. A cowboy owed some loyalty to the outfit he worked for; even a rank amateur who had missed his daily shave for the first time in years. Even though he wasn't being paid, there was a question of fidelity here. He was responsible for these cows. But he had no gun.

Studying the oncoming riders, Earl saw that one was a big man. Sid Vivian, he decided, and fought down an impulse to mount his horse and ride away. That would be desertion — a cowardly surrender to the dismay that was causing his heart to beat faster and faster. Recalling what he had told Jack Benteen, Earl repeated it now: "A man has to do what he thinks is right, regardless of the cost."

The words had sounded exactly right the other evening; but now, watching the three riders come toward him, they seemed flat and meaningless. In this dismal moment of waiting Earl wondered if all inspirational pronouncements sounded like that to the men they were meant for; if the editorials he wrote for the *Herald* were just useless echoes of impractical theory. Was physical prowess, and the courage that went with it, the important ingredient at times like this? Earl was considering that possibility, and being disheartened by it, when he identified Jack Benteen riding between Sid Vivian and Red Gillum.

What was this?

Neither Vivian nor Gillum held a gun. Yet Jack was riding with them. They weren't talking. All three of them were looking at him as they came on, and now Sid Vivian said to him harshly, "Mount up, Tipton. You're leaving."

"Leaving?"

Vivian nodded, and Red Gillum said amusedly, "You need a shave, Tipton. We're sending you to town for a shave."

A thin smile altered Sid Vivian's roan cheeks as he contemplated Earl. "What a cowboy!" he mused. Then he said with arrogant bluntness, "You and Jack are going to town right now."

Tipton looked at Benteen, not understanding this. "Are you quitting the gather?"

Benteen made an open-palmed gesture with his hands. "No choice," he said, quite matter-of-fact about it. "We're trespassing on Boxed W range and Sid says we've got to go."

"But that would be deserting Clay," Tipton protested. "We can't just ride off and let these cattle stray again."

Gillum loosed a hoot of jeering laughter. He winked at Sid and said, "Wouldn't that be awful, if these cows drifted off? I feel like crying, by God."

Vivian turned in the saddle and gave the brush a brief appraisal; then he said impatiently, "Mount up, Tipton, and ride out of here."

"But I couldn't do that," Earl said.

"Oh, yes, you can, and you're going to," Vivian announced angrily. Dismounting, he walked over to Earl and waggled a fist at him and asked, "Have you got to be showed?"

Earl peered at Benteen, who now said flatly, "Can't you see we've got no choice?"

"But they've no right to run us off like this," Earl insisted.

Sid Vivian cursed. "I'll show you who's got a right!" he shouted.

Earl saw it coming. He ducked Sid's big fist and struck out wildly. He hadn't consciously aimed at Vivian's nose, but the feel of smashed nostrils against his knuckles filled Earl with an exultant sense of achievement. He had hit Sid Vivian!

Astonished that this was so, Earl glanced at the knuckles of his right hand. There was blood on them.

Vivian's astonishment was as great as Tipton's. He wiped his nose on the back of a huge hand. He glanced at the blood, then gawked at Tipton in bug-eyed disbelief. "Why, you goddamn dude!" he snarled.

And then he slugged Tipton with successive rights and lefts, grunting with each hard swing.

When Tipton collapsed, Red called, "Stomp him, Sid!"

Vivian turned to Benteen. "Take his pony's reins." He hoisted Tipton into the saddle, then said, "Grab holt of him, and when he wakes up tell him he's lucky to be alive."

Leaving Boxed W, Spain angled back across the ridge. The brindle cow wouldn't be worth a damn as evidence. Spain cursed, understanding how Sid Vivian had rigged his wholesale thievery. There was no way to prove this cow wasn't one of the 250 that Lew Wade had purchased. But he was going to claim her, regardless. Taking care not to spook the brindle and her calf, he drove them toward Cartridge Creek.

Presently, as he crossed an open flat where greasewood grew sparsely, Spain noticed fresh tracks pointing southward; two shod horses. Backtrailing the hoofprints for a little distance, he observed the angle of approach and decided that these two riders had come from the direction of West Tank. Vivian and Gillum, he guessed, headed for Cartridge Creek to take a look-see. Spain studied the hoof cups, wanting to establish how recently they'd been made. There had been a slight breeze blowing from the west this morning; seeing the film of dust across the shoe marks, he remembered that the breeze had died over an hour ago. These tracks had been made before that.

Returning to the brindle cow and her calf, Spain hazed them over a series of rock benches that tilted upward to form the north bank of Big Arroyo. Vivian, he thought, probably wanted to check on the number of Roman Six cows that had been gathered. It would be like Sid to wait until the job was almost completed, then stage a night raid that would scatter the cows to hell and gone. Spain thought, We'll pull out for Purdy's place this evening. There probably wasn't another Roman Six cow to be found, anyway, and Vivian would know that if he tallied the held bunch.

When Spain rimmed out above Big Arroyo he peered southward. He saw no riders, but he did see something else that brought a curse to his lips: a considerable dust haze ten or twelve miles to the southeast.

"The dirty bastards!" he exclaimed, understanding instantly what the dust meant.

His first impulse was to ride fast toward the signal of trouble. But the trip would take almost an hour. The damage had already been done. No doubt about that. The dust was diminishing now; it formed a tawny banner that raveled out in a dissolving smear above the brush. The held herd had been scattered.

When Spain followed the cow and calf down the first steep slant into the arroyo, most of the dust was gone. "And so are the cows," he muttered.

Earl Tipton, he supposed, was on his way to town. It wouldn't have taken much to run him off. Spain cursed himself for not having left the Winchester with Earl, but it occurred to him that the newspaperman wouldn't have had the courage to use it. This gather had been a loco deal all along. The cards had been stacked against him from the moment Gus Jubal sold out to Boxed W. Spain wondered about Jack Benteen. The bartender hadn't much liked this proposition; he wouldn't have put up a fight, either. A fine pair, those two.

It took half an hour to cross the arroyo and climb out. When Spain rimmed the south bank there was no more dust. During the next hour he picked up five wild-eyed cows, and later, as he neared the holding ground, he observed a liberal sprinkling of horse tracks in the hoof-pocked pattern of cow tracks. Soon after that he came upon the two hobbled pack mules, one of which had got snagged in a mesquite thicket during the stampede. Dismounting, Spain freed the mule by unbuckling its hobble strap.

At sundown, as he hazed six cows and four calves onto the trampled flats north of Cartridge Creek, Spain smelled smoke. Halting at once, he peered toward camp and glimpsed a fragile streamer of wood smoke above the brush.

Spain drew his gun and eased his horse off at an angle. Warily circling, he wondered if Earl had started a supper fire before the raid, and could think of no reason why he should have. But if Vivian and Gillum had remained here after scattering the cows, why would they deliberately advertise their presence?

Baffled, Spain continued to circle. Because the need for reprisal was strong in him, he hoped that they were waiting — that he would have an opportunity to shoot it out here and now. But no sound or sign of movement disturbed the stillness as he halted at the creek.

The campfire was quite plain now, its flame making a fragile beacon against the deepening dusk. In this continuing silence Spain heard the cows moving toward water.

Six cows left out of 250; out of the thousand head that had left the Río Pantano.

Finally Spain called, "Hello the camp!"

For a long moment there was no answer. Then: "Is that you, Clay?"

Recognizing Earl Tipton's voice, Spain called, "Yes."

Riding toward the campfire and seeing Earl come out of the brush, Spain thought, So you ran off and hid while the cows were scattered.

But presently, peering at Earl's bruised and swollen face, Spain demanded, "What happened to you?"

Tipton told him about the brief fist fight, and how he had ridden back to camp alone after Benteen had refused to return. "Jack said it was no use," Earl reported. "He said nobody could buck Boxed W and hope to win."

"Then why did you come back?" Spain asked.

Tipton shrugged. "It seemed wrong to desert you at a time like this, even though the cows were gone." Then an oddly satisfied grin altered his scarred, whisker-bristled face. "Sid Vivian knocked me out," he said, and gently fingered a raw bruise on his jaw. "But I hit him once, Clay. I hit Sid Vivian. I gave him a bloody nose."

And while Spain absorbed that startling announcement, Earl added, "That's the first time I ever hit anyone. It was the queerest thing. I didn't plan to swing at Vivian. It was a spontaneous reaction. I struck without thinking." He chuckled in the lusty way of a man relishing a fond memory. "It gave me more satisfaction than anything I've ever done, Clay. It made me feel like a real man."

"You are," Spain said, admiring him and marveling that this should be so. "You're more of a man than Jack Benteen will ever be."

That pleased Tipton. He chuckled again and stood straighter than Spain had ever seen him stand before. "Wait until Eve hears about this," he said. "She'll think I've reverted to the savage instincts of a cave man."

"And she'll be tickled pink," Spain predicted.

"Tickled?"

Spain nodded. Wanting to impress Earl with this, he said thoughtfully, "Women like a little savagery in their men. Even respectable, educated women. Hasn't that ever occurred to you?"

"Well, yes," Earl admitted. "I've sensed it in Eve, but there didn't seem to be anything I could do about it."

Spain laughed at him. He said, "That's because you never hit anyone. Never gave anyone a bloody nose. But you have now — and your wife will be proud of you."

"Do you really think so, Clay?"

"I'm sure of it, if you'll just act proud of yourself," Spain assured him.

Unsaddling his horse, Spain appraised the flame-lit camp and understood that some of the cows had been run through here; most of them, by the look of it. Two bedrolls were trampled to tattered rags, a pack saddle had been splintered, and the contents of all four kyacks had been dumped on the ground.

"I was picking things up when you arrived," Earl said.

Using a hoof-trampled skillet and what other utensils could be salvaged, he began preparing supper.

It wasn't much of a meal, for little remained in the way of provisions. And because three days of hard riding had been wasted, Spain didn't relish his supper.

"Do you think Vivian will come back tonight?" Earl asked.

"Wish he would," Spain muttered. Observing the instant concern that came to Tipton's face, he added, "Don't let it fret you, Earl. Vivian did what he came here to do. He won't be back."

For a time then they sat staring into the fire's glowing embers, each lost in his own thoughts. Finally Earl asked, "Is there any way you could keep Vivian from scattering your cows if you gathered them again?"

Spain shrugged, and gave his attention to shaping a cigarette. "Might be, if I had men to do the gathering while I rode patrol."

"How could you stop a raid?"

"By shooting at any Boxed W man that crossed Big Arroyo," Spain said.

Tipton thought that over while he filled a brier pipe; when he had it drawing to suit him he said, "There's more than a herd of cattle involved, Clay. It's bigger than that. This is the first time anyone has stood up to Boxed W. If Lew Wade wins out, no one else will ever try to stop him."

"It's not Wade. Lew owns the ranch, but Vivian runs it to suit himself. I don't know why, but Lew is afraid of Sid. He admitted it to me this afternoon."

"Why, that's what Lace has been saying all along!" Earl exclaimed. "But it seemed utterly fantastic. I couldn't believe it."

Spain nodded. Recalling his own disbelief, he said, "Lace Fayette is a smart woman. Seems odd. Beauty and brains seldom go together."

"Oh, but you're wrong about that," Earl

said. "History is filled with beautiful women who had superior intellects." Shyly, in the fashion of a man not given to bragging, he added, "My wife is beautiful, and she has a good mind."

And an itch for men, Spain thought.

Afterward, when they shared the remaining bedroll, Earl asked, "Shall we drive the six cows to Purdy's place in the morning?"

Spain nodded, and, thinking how sorry a gather it was, said cynically, "Some roundup."

"Then what?"

"Well, I don't know just how it's going to be done, or how long it will take, but I'm going to collect two hundred and forty-four cows from Boxed W."

"Good!" Earl exclaimed.

Spain snorted, "What's good about it?"

"Why, your refusal to give up — your determination to end Boxed W's domination of Apache Basin."

Spain grunted disgustedly. He said, "I don't give a damn about that, one way or the other. All I want is my cattle. And by God, I'm going to get them."

CHAPTER FIFTEEN

There was a distinct chill in the air this morning, a sharp coldness that caused Spain to hold his palms to Earl's breakfast fire. Presently turning to warm his shanks, Spain gazed across the sunless flats, observing the tawny color of mesquite beans dangling high up where cattle couldn't reach them. A row of cottonwoods on a far bend of Cartridge Creek had turned yellow during the past few days, and Spain thought, Soon be winter.

Earl hummed a tune as he prepared breakfast. His morning cheerfulness was a surprising thing to Spain. Most of the men he had known were grouchy until they had had coffee of a morning. But Earl seemed to wake up smiling. Observing him now, and admiring him, Spain marveled at the change in his own attitude; a few days ago he had looked upon this scholarly man with casual contempt.

It was well after sunup when they left Cartridge Creek. Easing along behind the six cows, four calves, and two pack mules, Spain announced cynically, "Abilene, here we come!"

Earl grinned at him. "Not much of a trail herd, is it?"

Presently Earl took out after a bunch-quitter cow and turned it back. Riding along beside Spain again, he confided, "I like this better than anything I've ever done. Feel better, too."

Contemplating Earl's tanned, fist-scarred face, Spain said, "Your wife won't recognize you. She'll think you're some tough drifter wanting a woman."

That amused Earl. "Tough drifter," he reflected. He thought about it for a moment. "That's how I feel. A trifle tough."

"And wanting a woman?"

Earl nodded. Smiling sheepishly, he admitted, "I can scarcely wait to get home."

Spain laughed at him. "Three days without seeing a shemale and you've got romantic fever. Now you know how cowboys feel when they hit town once a month."

Earl nodded. "I understand it, Clay, but I wonder if Eve will."

"For sure," Spain said confidently. Guessing how it had been between them, he said,

"Some wives need lots of attention. Especially the warm-blooded ones. They like a honeyfussing husband."

The bunch-quitter cow took off into the brush again and Earl galloped after her. He rode surprisingly well for a man who'd never earned his pay asaddle. Watching Earl turn the cow back, Spain wondered what Eve Tipton's reaction would be when she learned that Earl had stood up to Sid Vivian while Benteen had run off like a spooked jack rabbit.

They were within five miles of Purdy's place when Joe Pratt angled around the driven cows and announced, "Lace Fayette sent me to help you, Clay."

"So?"

The little rider seemed wholly repentant. He said, "I shouldn't of let Gus talk me into sellin' my cows. It wasn't the right thing to do. But I had an awful itch for a spree in town."

"You broke?" Spain asked.

"Flatter'n a pannycake," Joe admitted. "Gus robbed me." Then he said, "Miss Fayette promised to pay me real good wages for helping with her half of the cows."

Spain introduced him to Tipton. He said thoughtfully, "If I had one man more, we could start gathering day after tomorrow."

"Couldn't three of us handle it?" Earl asked.

Spain nodded. "But it would take a long time, and you've got a wife to look after."

"I'll do that tonight," Earl said with matter-of-fact confidence. "I could be back tomorrow evening."

Spain asked, "You mean it, Earl?"

"Of course I do, and for as long as it takes to get those two hundred and forty-four cows."

"Even if there's some shooting?"

Earl nodded. "I'll borrow a Winchester in town."

Spain grinned at him. He said, *"Bueno!"*

Then, as Joe Pratt rode along with them, Spain suggested, "Go on into town now, Earl. We can handle this little jag of cows."

Earl was eager as a man could be, but he asked, "You sure you won't need me, Clay?"

"Positive," Spain assured him, and when Earl eased around the cows, he called, "Be sure to tell your wife about giving Sid Vivian a bloody nose."

Watching Tipton ride off, Pratt said, "So that's the galoot Benteen told about in town. Said he hit Vivian and got hisself knocked colder'n a frozen cow flop, but wouldn't quit regardless."

"That's Earl," Spain said. "Less savvy and

187

more guts than a bloated bull in an alfalfa patch."

Gail Purdy was hanging out a wash when she saw Earl Tipton come along the road. Going quickly to the gate, she called, "Where's Clay?"

"Coming with the cows," Earl reported, not stopping.

"But Jack Benteen said the gather was stampeded."

"It was. Clay has only six cows and four calves." Riding on, Earl called over his shoulder, "We're going to start a new roundup day after tomorrow."

Smiling now, Gail returned to the clothesline. She had worried about Clay. Fearing he was hurt, she had been tempted to go looking for him. The knowledge that he was all right, and would soon be here, whipped up an urgent sense of anticipation. Gail wondered about that, asking herself why it should be so. Clay Spain was obviously in love with Lace Fayette. And he resented being involved with Sam's trouble. He had shown that plainly enough; had frankly admitted it.

She was peeling potatoes on the kitchen stoop when Spain and Pratt came in from the flats south of the yard. Clay's whisker-shagged face seemed even more gaunt than usual and he looked tired, but a devil-be-damned grin rutted his cheeks as he introduced Joe Pratt. Then he asked, "Mind if we hook up that water pipe to the tank?"

"Go right ahead," Gail said. "You'll find tools in the barn."

Afterward, when the job was done and Pratt had fixed up makeshift bunks in the barn, Spain came to the lamp-lit kitchen. "How's Sam?" he asked.

"Well, he hates being in jail, of course. But it will soon be over. His trial starts tomorrow morning."

"He should be turned loose by noon," Spain predicted. As he watched her work at the stove, it occurred to him that Gail had never seemed so pretty. There was something different about her oval face; more color in her cheeks.

Spain chuckled, guessing that the hot stove caused that. But there was more to it than the heightened color. It was a sense of buoyancy that came from her, and a stimulating man-woman awareness so strong that he felt like taking her in his arms.

As if sharing that awareness, and being embarrassed by it, Gail said censuringly, "Don't gawk at me, Clay."

"Why not?"

"Well, I'm liable to spill something." Smiling secretively, she asked, "Do you like my hair this way?"

"Is it different?"

Gail sighed and gave her attention to the boiling potatoes.

Spain contemplated her hair. Lamplight gave it a soft sheen, bringing out rich chestnut tones in the tightly braided bun at the nape of her neck. Finally he asked, "Didn't you part it on the side before?"

She nodded, not speaking until he asked, "Why the change to a middle part?"

Then she said soberly, "I thought you might like it better."

Spain wondered if there were some reason he should prefer it this way. Women did the damnedest things for the damnedest reasons. Watching her fork beef into a skillet, he understood that Gail was an attractive young woman; more attractive than most of the girls that had found husbands in Apache Basin, where pretty girls were few and far between.

"Must be lots of men with poor eyesight in this country," he mused.

"Why do you say that?"

"Well, seems odd you're not married."

Gail turned to look at him, her eyes calmly appraising, her long lips composed and unsmiling. "What's so odd about it?" she asked.

"I can't understand why some man hasn't toted you off to a preacher," Spain said. Deliberately studying her now, he added, "Sound of mind and limb. Built the way a woman should be, and a good cook."

"Why, thank you," she said, and curtsied gracefully. Then she asked, "Doesn't it occur to you that I might not have met a man I'd care to marry?"

Joe Pratt came to the stoop with a lantern. "Riders coming down the road," he announced. "Three or four, by the sound."

"Put out that lantern," Spain commanded. Going outside, he stepped clear of the doorway lamplight and listened to a faint thudding west of the yard. The horses were moving at a fast trot. As they crossed the dry wash, the sound of travel faded, then came again as they neared the yard. There were three, by the sound. Spain thought, Vivian, Gillum, and Wade.

He said to Pratt, "Ease back toward the barn," and Joe drifted across the dark yard.

Spain chuckled, wholly pleased. This would be some different from those other times when Boxed W had come into this yard. Temper rose in him, and an old eagerness quickened his pulse. Yet even now, welcoming all this, he couldn't understand why Sid Vivian should make such a stupid play. Sid probably didn't know about Pratt, but it seemed odd that Vivian should come here tonight.

Spain had his gun out and cocked when he realized that the horses were not turning in at the gate — that they were passing the yard. In this moment, with the urge to force a play spreading through him, Spain had the impulse to call out and challenge the three riders. He resisted the impulse, but now, listening to the diminishing sound of hoofbeats, he felt tense and irritable.

Going back to the house, he said to Gail, "I thought they were coming here."

"Probably going to town so as to be on hand for the trial tomorrow morning," she said. Observing the scowl on his face, she asked wonderingly, "You sorry they didn't come into the yard?"

Spain nodded. He said, "This time I was set for them."

But Joe Pratt wasn't sorry. "No sense facing trouble until trouble faces you," he said cheerfully.

Afterward, as they ate supper, Joe asked, "We going to town for provisions tomorrow?"

"I am," Spain said. Looking at Gail, he

added, "If you'll let me borrow your wagon, I'll bring out a good supply of groceries."

"I'll ride with you," she agreed. "And perhaps Sam will be coming home with us."

Joe asked, "What about me, Clay?"

"You stay here," Spain said. "You've had your spree."

Three boys were perched on the cattle-pen fence when Earl Tipton rode into Hondo. One of them called, "Hello, Mr. Tipton."

Surprised at such friendliness, Earl peered up at them, and now another boy asked, "Is it true what they're saying, Mr. Tipton?"

"What are they saying?" Earl asked.

"That you punched Sid Vivian in the nose."

"Why, yes," Earl admitted.

The boys stared at him in awe-struck wonder. One of them asked, "Which fist did you hit him with?"

"My right," Earl said. Observing the admiration in their eyes, he sat straight in the saddle and announced, "I gave Vivian a bloody nose."

He rode on then, basking in the warmth of a new-found pride. It hadn't occurred to him that Jack Benteen would tell about his hitting Sid Vivian. Eve probably knew about it too. He wondered if Clay Spain were correct in believing she would be proud of him.

Two men hailed him with friendly greetings as he rode along Main Street; when he passed the blacksmith shop in Shiloh Alley, Jules Huffmeyer called, "Welcome home, slugger!"

Jules had never been friendly, and Earl wondered if there were some secret derision in the greeting, a sly commentary on the fact that he'd been knocked out by Vivian. But that doubt was dissolved when Cap Ledbetter shook his hand and exclaimed, "You did something a lot of men have wanted to do for a long time!"

When Earl walked back to Main Street from the livery, Lace Fayette called to him from the bank doorway, and while he was telling her about Spain's plans for another roundup, Sheriff Ed Kenyon came over from the courthouse.

"Vivian had no right to jump you like he did," Ed said gravely. "I'm glad you got in one good punch."

It was the same as he walked along Residential Avenue. Even some of the ladies smiled at him from verandas, and that, Earl thought, was a good sign. If they approved of his brief brawling, perhaps Eve would also.

She did.

Coming out to meet him on the veranda, Eve cried, "Earl, darling!" and came into his arms with an eagerness that astonished him.

Pleased and excited, Earl remembered what Clay Spain had told him. Fairly lifting her off her feet, he kissed her hard and hungrily, not stopping until she struggled for release.

When they went into the house he kissed her again and hugged her so tightly she squealed.

Eve fought clear of his arms. But she was smiling, and now she exclaimed, "You've changed so, I can scarcely believe it!"

Earl grinned at her. "Haven't shaved since I left," he bragged.

"It's not just that, Earl. It's something else. You seem like a different person."

"Like a man?"

Eve nodded.

"That's how I feel," Earl said, and escorted her into the bedroom.

CHAPTER SIXTEEN

Saddle horses, teams, and single rigs lined hitch racks when Spain drove into Hondo with Gail. It was shortly before nine o'clock and a considerable crowd was in front of the courthouse.

"Looks like everybody and his brother has come for the trial," Spain reflected. Observing the large number of women, he added, "And his sister, too."

Gail hadn't talked much on the trip. She didn't seem apprehensive or nervous. It was as if there just was nothing to say. When he had complimented her on the powder-blue dress and little black pancake hat, Gail merely shrugged; now she said quietly, "I'll be glad when it's over."

"Shouldn't take the jury more than ten minutes, once Judge Fickett gives them the case," Spain predicted. Halting the team, he said, "Bring Sam to the hotel for dinner. I'm buying."

Gail climbed down and smiled up at him. "I hope he's free by then."

"No doubt about it." Noticing that her hair was parted on the side today, he asked, "Why did you change back your hair-do?"

Gail made an open-palmed gesture of resignation. "It was just an idea," she murmured. "A silly idea."

"Why was it silly?"

"Because I was trying to look like someone else."

"Who?" Spain asked, baffled.

But now Earl Tipton and his wife came up, arm in arm, and Eve said pleasantly, "Come along, Gail, or you won't get a seat."

They started along the walk, and Spain turned into the Mercantile wagon yard.

When he had tied the team to a ring in the loading platform, Spain walked out to Main Street. Doc Randall came down the outside stairway from his office and untied a horse at the hitch rack. Coming abreast of him now, Spain said, "So you miss the trial."

"Babies don't wait on trials," Randall muttered, a deep scowl matching the gruffness of his voice. Getting into the buggy, he sighed, "That nester settlement on Shirttail Flats will be a bigger town than Hondo at the rate they're breeding. Five babies born in the past three weeks, and two more about due." Then he said confidentially, "Watch out for Bob Teague. He's got an itch."

"To shoot me?"

Randall nodded.

"Just talk, most likely."

"No, it's more than that. Teague cried while I dug out that slug. He swore he'd shoot you down like a dog."

"So?" Spain mused, and glanced at the hotel. "Teague still in town?"

Doc nodded.

"Able to walk?"

"A little, with crutches."

Randall backed his rig away from the hitch rack. "Mind what I say about keeping your eyes open," he warned.

Spain watched Randall drive along Main Street. Teague, he supposed, was attending the trial, along with Wade, Vivian, and Gillum. He thought, Four of them against me, and then muttered, "No, just three." Wade didn't count.

Quartering across Main Street toward the courthouse, Spain observed that the crowd had gone inside, and the door was closed. He wondered if Sam's trial would really be as short as he had predicted it would be. The jury might take a little time, just to make it look right, but there seemed no doubt what the verdict would be. Jurors who knew Sam Purdy would not be impressed by Lew Wade's feeble fabrication about coincidence, or Vivian's bald charge that Lin Graham had been shot without warning or provocation.

Spain was halfway across the street when a man in an upstairs hotel window called his name. Not loudly or sharply, but with a pleased, almost gleeful voice that gave Spain no warning until he saw the gun in Bob Teague's hand.

"Make your grab," Teague said, a mirthless grin rutting his sallow cheeks as he leaned farther out the window and waggled the gun.

Spain understood that the slightest movement of his right arm would be a signal to Bob Teague to pull the trigger.

"Maybe I don't want to grab," Spain said, forcing a casual drawl, revealing none of the tension in him.

Teague chuckled. "Makes no never mind to me," he said, plainly relishing this moment. "You're a gone goose either way."

Spain had seen hate in a man's eyes, and the hot urge to kill; but he had never before seen what was in Teague's eyes now: a witless staring that was like a metallic shine — a blank, unblinking gaze that held no expression at all.

"You're loco," Spain said, and turned as if intending to retreat across the street. At this same instant, as Teague scoffed, "You ain't going no place," Spain drew his gun.

Teague fired, and the bullet passed so close to Spain's face that he dodged instinctively, and so was in motion when Teague's gun exploded a second time. Crouched sideways to make a thinner target, Spain fired up at the window and continued to shoot until Teague collapsed across the sill. Teague's gun slid from nerveless fingers, its thud on the plank walk sounding quite loud against the street's sudden stillness. A crimson stain slid down Teague's left cheek and ran into his hair.

The courthouse door opened. A man rushed out, shouting, "What's happened?"

While Spain ejected four spent shells from his pistol, a general exodus from the courtroom began.

Cap Ledbetter called, "Who'd you shoot at, Clay?"

Spain jabbed a thumb toward the upstairs window. He was reloading his gun when Red Gillum exclaimed, "It's Bob Teague!" and ran into the hotel.

Lace Fayette came out of the crowd to ask excitedly, "What happened, Clay?"

The question irritated Spain. Wasn't it

plain enough, with blood dripping from Teague's down-tilted head? Why did people always ask such damn-fool questions at a time like this? The street was crowded now. People watched Gillum lift Teague out of the window; they peered at the pool of blood on the sidewalk and all of them seemed to be talking at once.

Sheriff Kenyon came toward him, with Earl Tipton, Eve, and Gail close behind. "Why'd you shoot Teague?" Kenyon demanded harshly.

"A damn-fool question," Spain said with equal harshness.

Temper flared in Kenyon's eyes. "Don't sass me, Clay. I won't take it!"

"Shouldn't you go see if Teague is dead?" Lace Fayette suggested in a soothing, gracious voice, and now Sid Vivian called from across the street, "Anybody seen Doc Randall?"

Earl Tipton had disappeared; his wife stood nearby with Gail. Spain hadn't noticed Lew Wade in the crowd, but now he saw him hurry into the hotel, and at that moment Gillum shouted from the window, "Bob is dead!"

"Did Teague shoot first?" Kenyon asked.

Spain nodded.

"Well, what started it? How'd you get to

shooting at each other?"

Sid Vivian elbowed his way through the crowd. He commanded, "Arrest him, Ed. The charge is murder."

"But Clay says Teague fired first," Kenyon said, plainly reluctant and wanting time to think this out. "A man has a right to defend himself."

Someone in the crowd announced, "Teague threatened to shoot Spain on sight. I heard him say it."

"Is this street a court?" Vivian asked disgustedly. "I say you're to arrest him, Ed."

Spain had finished reloading his pistol, but he hadn't holstered it. He saw Kenyon glance at the weapon, and observed a fleeting alteration in the Sheriff's eyes; something that might have been doubt, or fear, or an old man's regret for lost courage.

"I'll take that gun," Kenyon said, and reached for it.

Spain said, "No, Ed," and backed out into the street far enough so that there was no one behind him.

"You can't arrest him for defending himself," Cap Ledbetter said. "That's no crime, Ed."

And another man shouted, "Why should Spain be arrested if Teague shot first?"

Red Gillum came striding through the

crowd, his freckled face ashine with perspiration. "If Spain said that, he lied!"

"What you mean?" Kenyon demanded.

"Bob was alive when I got there," Gillum reported. "He used his dying breath to say Spain fired first."

In this moment it seemed to Spain that every person in the street stared at him in silent accusation. The pressure of those eyes was like a physical impact. He peered across ten feet of dust at Gillum, who now stood beside Kenyon and he said, "You're a liar, Red."

"Holster your gun and call me that!" Gillum taunted.

Sid Vivian stepped in front of Gillum, pushing him back. He said to Kenyon, "Who you going to believe — a known troublemaker, or the testimony of a dying man?"

That did it. Spain saw the decision in Kenyon's eyes as Ed announced, "I've got to arrest you, Clay."

"Lynching is what he deserves!" Red Gillum shouted.

Ignoring that, Kenyon stepped forward. "Hand me your gun."

"And get myself lynched?"

"Give me that gun," Kenyon commanded, "or I'll take it away from you!"

"Wait a moment," Earl Tipton called, and he came through the crowd with two small boys. "These youngsters witnessed the fight. They were up in a tree and saw the whole thing."

"What's that got to do with it?" Vivian objected.

But Kenyon asked, "Did you boys see who shot first?"

They both nodded, and one of them said, "The man in the window."

"You sure?" Kenyon asked.

"Yes, sir. He shot two times and then the other man started shooting."

A gusty sigh slid from Ed Kenyon's lips. He said, "Thank you, boys." Turning to look at Lew Wade, who now stood with Vivian and Gillum, he said, "That's proof Spain shot in self-defense. Too bad it happened, but I want no trouble over it."

Wade nodded agreement. He appeared dazed and unable to comprehend the turn of events that had resulted in the death of another Boxed W rider. But now, as Earl, his wife, Lace, and Gail moved out to stand beside Spain, Sid Vivian exclaimed, "There'll be trouble, by God! You can count on that. If the law won't handle it, Boxed W will."

Spain saw the impact of that ultimatum tighten Ed Kenyon's eyes. The Sheriff peered briefly at Vivian, then shifted his glance to Wade. "I hold you accountable for what your crew does, Lew. I want no more trouble." Then he announced, "Court will resume in fifteen minutes."

All at once then Spain was besieged by men who wanted to shake his hand — meek-eyed homesteaders who had been dominated by Boxed W, admiring townsmen who resented Vivian's hell-raising riders. Embarrassed by this attention, Spain welcomed Kenyon's shouted announcement: "Courtroom door will be closed in ten minutes!"

As the crowd thinned out, Spain shook hands with Earl Tipton, saying, "Much obliged for those witnesses, *amigo*."

Jack Benteen came up and said, "How about a drink on me?"

"Good idea," Spain said, eager to get off this street.

But Earl protested, "How about the ladies?"

"We'll excuse you," Lace Fayette said graciously.

As the women turned toward the courthouse, Gail said, "Watch out for Red Gillum, Clay."

Spain grinned at her; he said, "Red better watch out for me."

■ ■ ■ ■

The jury reached a verdict shortly before noon: "Not guilty."

There was a spontaneous burst of applause, and Lace Fayette exclaimed happily, "No one will be afraid of Boxed W now!"

As if in proof of that prediction, three men from Shirttail Flats — Seth Arbuckle, Pete Seely, and Bert Ingram — offered to help Spain with his roundup. A fourth man, Pinky Troop, promised to join the gather as soon as his wife had her baby, which he said would be within the week.

Sam Purdy shook Spain's hand with a tight-fingered sincerity, saying, "I'll be helping you, too, Clay."

And Earl Tipton predicted confidently, "We'll have those two hundred and forty-four cows in no time at all!"

But Spain knew it wouldn't be that easy.

CHAPTER SEVENTEEN

It took three days to establish a well-provisioned camp at Cartridge Creek. During that time a *remuda* of seventeen horses was collected, a chuck wagon rigged up, and considerable firewood gathered. When Pinky Troop arrived late in the afternoon of the third day he said wonderingly, "Looks like you boys intend to stay till Christmas."

"A week at the most," Earl Tipton predicted.

Even Sam Purdy was optimistic. "We can match Boxed W, man for man, not counting the line-camp riders."

The three homesteaders made quite a to-do over Troop's announcement that his wife had given birth to another girl baby.

"Three girls in a row," Bert Ingram gibed. "What you got in mind, Pinky — a harem?"

And Pete Seely, father of two boys, bragged joyfully, "Doc Randall says it takes a man to make a man."

Supper, prepared by Seely and Ingram, was a cheerful affair. Watching these men and listening to their jovial talk, Spain suspected they had no real understanding of what this deal might mean. To hear them laugh and gossip, you'd think they were attending a community barbecue that would wind up in a dance. Unlike Joe Pratt, who was morosely silent this evening, they hadn't fought their way out of Sonora; hadn't seen riderless horses with blood-smeared saddles in the cheerless dawn. To them this was a welcome break in the hard-scrabble monotony of homestead toil — an opportunity to ride risky trails with stalwart companions. Somebody might get hurt, but that was a hazy, impersonal aspect that gave the gather a spicy flavor. Long obedient to Sid Vivian's domination, they glowed now with a new and expansive confidence; banded together and feeling strong for the first time, they were mentally thumbing their noses at Boxed W.

Seth Arbuckle, a loud-mouthed man of indeterminate age, announced, "I've took sass from them smart alecks aplenty. I've stood on my own doorstep and listened to talk that spoilt my vittles for a week. But now, by grab, the tune will be played a different way!"

Spain thought, More different than you realize, and wondered if Arbuckle would stand up under fire. He doubted it.

As if sharing that opinion, Joe Pratt mumbled, "Maybe they won't be so cocky this time tomorrow night."

Spain shrugged. "You still feeling the effects of that spree in town, Joe?"

"Not the drinking," Joe said.

"Being robbed by Gus?"

Joe shook his head. "A woman. The sweetest-smellin' blonde woman I ever saw. Name of Lilybelle. She acted like I was the best thing had happened to her in a long, long time. Like me and her was a perfect match."

"Change her mind?"

Joe nodded. "Soon as she found out I was broke."

Spain grinned at him. "That shouldn't surprise you, Joe. The sporty ones always do you like that."

"But she was something special," Pratt said, dejected as a man could be. Turning his back to the fire, he added softly, "She still is."

The world, Spain thought, was full of trouble. And women were mixed up in most of it, one way or another. Take this deal, for instance. If Lace Fayette hadn't sweet-talked him into siding Sam Purdy, there'd have been no trouble with Boxed W. He smiled, recalling Lace's elation after Sam's acquittal. She had told Lew Wade to his face that Boxed W was through bossing Apache Basin. Predicting that the irrigation project would be started within a week, Lace had taken the afternoon stage for Tucson to hire a construction crew.

Earl Tipton brought his filled plate around the fire and squatted beside Spain. "Going to be a trifle chilly tonight," he said.

Presently he asked, "You think there'll be some shooting before this is over, Clay?"

"Suppose."

Earl thought about that for a moment before saying, "I've never shot at a human being. It will be a new experience for me — and not very pleasant." Then, as if convincing himself, he said soberly, "This isn't just to reclaim some stolen cattle, Clay. It's a crusade to make Apache Basin free, once and for all."

"Large order," Spain commented dryly.

"Those are the exact words Ed Kenyon used when I tried to explain it to him," Earl reflected. "He's an odd one, Ed is. Always talking against shooting. Seemed to have a mania against the use of firearms. Yet day before yesterday when I left Hondo I heard pistol shots in that arroyo west of the cattle pens, and found Ed down there firing away at a target. He had two guns strapped on, and was using the left one. He holstered it after each shot, then drew and fired."

"Have to call him Two-Gun Kenyon," Spain said, amused. "Ed say why he needed a left-hand gun?"

"No, but he seemed a trifle embarrassed."

Sam Purdy joined them now and asked, "How you planning to go about getting those cows, Clay?"

"Well, it will take time, but I think we'll do it like this," Spain said. Standing up, he announced, "Here's how it stacks up for tomorrow morning. I want four men to stand guard on the south rim of Big Arroyo, well spread out and staying high up where you can spot everything that comes this way from Boxed W."

He had already decided who those men would be, but now he took a moment to contemplate the firelit faces before saying, "Sam, you'll be in charge of that detail along with Earl, Arbuckle, and Troop. Two more men, Seely and Ingram, will guard camp and loose-herd the gather as it comes in."

While he took time to light a cigarette, Pratt asked, "How about you and me?"

"We'll do the gathering, Joe. A few head at a time."

For a moment, while they thought it over, no one spoke. Then Earl asked, "Couldn't you use another man up front, Clay?"

"You?"

Tipton nodded and said eagerly, "Wouldn't that hurry things up, with three of us gathering cows?"

Spain grinned at him, appreciating the offer and the spirit in which it was made. But he said, "Speed won't mean a thing unless we keep what cows we get. That's where the pinch will come — hanging on to our gather."

Seth Arbuckle asked, "Why wouldn't it be better for all eight of us to just ride into Boxed W and demand those cows?"

Looking at this raw-boned homesteader, Spain thought, A grandstander for sure. He had no confidence in him. He asked quietly, "Suppose Sid Vivian said no?"

"Well . . ." Arbuckle began; then, as if abruptly visualizing what that would mean, he was silent.

Spain let it ride for a long moment, wanting them all to savor the raw taste of the thing. Then he warned, "Don't think Vivian won't fight to keep those cows. Don't get it into your heads that eight men can spook

Boxed W. This won't be fun, once the shooting starts. You'd better understand that now."

His warning sobered them. For a little interval there was no sound save the low crackle of a burning mesquite log. A vagrant breeze, sharp with night's coldness, fanned the fire into bright flame so that the grave and thoughtful faces were fully revealed.

Observing their gravity, Spain guessed that now, for the first time, these men understood what was ahead of them. They weren't banded together now. They were individuals, each alone with his private apprehensions.

Seth Arbuckle was probably remembering that he had a wife wholly dependent upon him — a clinging-vine type of woman who'd be helpless as a widow. Pinky Troop would be thinking about his three little girls, wondering who would feed them if he were crippled or killed. And Pete Seely had two small boys to think about. It would be the same with Bert Ingram, who had a large family, and Sam Purdy, with a sister to support.

There wasn't much doubt what was in Earl Tipton's mind, Spain reflected. Earl, more sensitive than any of them, would be dreading the moment when he might have to shoot at a man. Earl wouldn't be much concerned with what happened to him in a physical way; what he feared most was being afraid.

Attempting to shrug off an increasing depression, Spain thought, If we have some luck it may not be bad. But he couldn't discard a nagging sense of responsibility, and so he said, "Let's get this straight. I didn't ask you boys into my fight with Boxed W. You owe me no favors, and I want no favors. If you're helping me because you want to take a crack at Boxed W on your own account, all right. But not as a favor to me."

Sam Purdy asked, "You wondering if we'll run out on you in a pinch, like Jack Benteen did?"

"No, not that. I mean it isn't too late to pull out now. Married men have wives to think about, and some of you have children." He grinned at Pratt, adding, "Joe and I are bachelors. We've just got ourselves to think about, which makes a difference."

"Damned sorry thinking," Joe muttered. Presently he added, "No reason to fight, and no reason not to. No reason for nothing."

Spain understood then how deeply disappointed he was, and felt sorry for him. Poor

Joe had found what he had thought was real love, and now he couldn't abide the knowledge that Lilybelle didn't want him at all; just his cash.

"I've got a reason to fight," Pete Seely announced.

"So?" Spain prompted.

Seely peered into the fire, an expression of infinite patience on his angular, flame-reddened face. He said thoughtfully, "I got two boys old enough to see things. And think things. They've saw Sid Vivian ride into my yard like he owned it. And they've heard him talk like I was dirt under his feet. Last month Red Gillum and two other Boxed W toughs drove a jag of cattle across my alfalfa patch. When I hollered at them, Red called me a yellow-bellied bastard. My wife heard it, and so did the boys."

He picked up a burning twig and lit his pipe. Then the resentment and anger of a man tortured by self-contempt altered his voice as he said harshly, "A man with growin' boys can't crawl on his belly forever. He's got to make up his mind to fight, or leave the country. My mind is made up."

Bert Ingram said, "Amen to that." Considerably older than Seely, he had the same look of long patience. "I've took talk that made me sick to my stomach afterward," he admitted.

Sam Purdy nodded, that silent admission of kindred shame reminding Spain of the first morning at Purdy's house.

"Me too," Arbuckle said.

As if seeking an excuse that might wash away all this mutual self-contempt, Pinky Troop suggested, "Maybe we just been waiting for a fair chance to fight — and now we've got it."

"That's it precisely!" Earl Tipton exclaimed. He smiled at Spain. "I told you this was more than a roundup. It's a crusade against injustice — against brutal domination."

Spain gave the faces a lingering attention; he asked, "Does that mean you're determined to go through with this deal?"

They nodded, and Seth Arbuckle bragged, "We ain't so spooky as you might think. Just slow to get started, is all."

Bert Ingram announced, "Coffee's still hot."

Some of the cheerfulness returned then. Seely came over to Spain and inquired, "What time you want breakfast ready?"

"Well, Joe and I will head out a trifle early — about four. The others can wait until daylight."

Moving over to where Sam Purdy was

warming his shanks, Spain asked, "You ridden that Big Arroyo country, Sam?"

"Some."

"You recall a deep saddle due south from Boxed W?"

Sam nodded.

"That's the most likely place for them to cross, coming this way."

"There's another saddle southwest, near the Mesa Parada," Sam said. "You figuring to cross there with the cattle?"

"Unless we run into trouble. In which case we might hit the arroyo anywhere at all."

Sam took out his pipe and tamped tobacco into it. He said, "I sure hope this deal goes over. It will mean a lot to all of us." Then, in the reluctant fashion of a shy man, he asked softly, "Is there an understanding between you and Lace Fayette?"

That question astonished Spain. It seemed fantastic that Sam Purdy, of all men, should be prying into his personal affairs. "You mean — have I asked her to marry me?" he demanded.

Sam nodded, and there was no mistaking the alertness in his eyes.

"No," Spain said. Seeing a slow smile alter Sam's face, he thought, You've got a case on her, sure as hell.

"I disliked to ask," Sam admitted. "But

I'm glad I did."

Afterward, snug in his bedroll, Spain wondered why so meek a man as Sam Purdy should have romantic notions about Lace Fayette. It hadn't occurred to him that there was any romance in Gail's bachelor brother; even now the idea of Sam's having amorous intentions seemed odd and out of character. But presently, as he recalled how swiftly and strongly he himself had been attracted to Lace Fayette, Spain's bafflement vanished. Lace had a way with her that could make any man itch.

CHAPTER EIGHTEEN

Starlight gave the frost-coated ground a vague tinseled shine when Spain and Pratt crossed the sandy bottom of Big Arroyo an hour before dawn. There was no wind in this high-walled slot, but the damp dead cold here seemed more penetrating.

"Might be in for an early winter," Spain said, and hoped it wouldn't come too soon.

Pratt rode slumped deep into the up-turned collar of his mackinaw. "Wish I'd bought me a sheep-lined coat before I went broke," he mumbled. "And some wool socks."

The frost disappeared as they climbed to higher ground. When they rimmed out on top, a brisk wind came off the towering Barricades and the cloud-banked sky to the west was dark. Quartering past Boxed W, where one lamplit window made a faint beacon, they approached West Tank at first daylight. Spain set a faster pace now, eager to get this raid started. By the look of things, most of the rebranded Roman Six herd was on these flats, and he predicted cheerfully, "Here's where the Spain boy gets back into cow business!"

An ancient windmill clanked methodically above the shallow, breeze-ruffled water as they circled West Tank. Riding at a walk, they drove eleven cows and nine calves away from the marginal mud. When the cattle began moving southward in a compact bunch, Spain made swift, short circles, adding recruits along the way. In the first hour he choused sixteen more cows out of the brush. By the time they skirted Mesa Parada's prowlike west end, they were driving forty-seven cows, over thirty calves, and two bulls.

A damned good haul, Spain thought; but because he understood that this was probably the biggest they would make, he felt no real jubilation. Sid Vivian would have riders out, and it was just a matter of time before this deal was discovered. After that there'd be no easy hauls.

Leaving Joe to push the cattle along, Spain angled up the steep slope of Mesa Parada for a look-see. This was some eight or ten miles south of the route they had traveled earlier this morning, and thus that much farther from Boxed W. The eastern sky was clear, with the sun's warmth dissolving the last clots of frosty mist from low spots, but westward a great bank of dark clouds still cloaked Barricade Divide. As he observed this contrast, the thought came to Spain that everything in nature had its absolute opposite: warmth and cold, light and shadow, wet and dry, mountain and valley. A man's life was apt to be the same, a contrasting pattern of ups and downs, with the scales never coming into perfect balance.

Thinking of what had happened to him since leaving Sonora, Spain reflected that his luck could stand some improvement. About halfway up the mesa's slope he halted on a shelving rock outcrop to rest the bay gelding. From this elevation he had a clear view of the land northward to Boxed W's headquarters, which he identified by the remote shine of a windmill. There was no sign of travel in that vicinity, but an intervening ridge shut off the West Tank flats. Riding on up to the mesa's broad crest, Spain halted again, and now, with West Tank visible, he gave the brush-blotched land a probing appraisal. There was no dust or movement near the tank's dwarfed speck of sun-silvered water. Shortening the scope of his questing eyes, Spain studied mesquite flats and the gently rising land this side of them. No riders there, he decided, and was about to leave when a thin tendril of dust caught his attention.

Spain focused his eyes on that warning signal. Keeping a steady watch, he caught a glimpse of two riders crossing an open space in the brush, and judged the distance to be not more than half a mile. He thought, Now it starts, and loosed a dismal curse. This first raid had looked good a few minutes ago; it had seemed like a cinch. But not now.

Drawing his Winchester from the saddle scabbard, Spain spurred his horse into a reckless, sliding descent and shouted, "Crowd 'em a trifle, Joe!"

Pratt peered up at him, instantly alert. "Somebody comin'?"

"Two men, close," Spain reported. "You stay with the cattle."

Then he rode to the east end of the rock outcrop, gave it a hasty appraisal, and decided to make a stand here. It didn't offer much protection, but there was no time to look for a better place. There was one thing in its favor: He'd be high enough to see what was going on. Dismounting, Spain looped the reins over his left arm and wondered if this borrowed horse was gun-shy. Seeing two riders gallop out of brush a hundred yards away, he thought, I'll soon know.

When he fired, the bay shied, yanking him back. "Stand, you jughead!" Spain ordered, and watched both riders pull up. One of them, tall and black-bearded, he identified as being an old Boxed W hand named Linkervale; the other, a blocky, round-faced man, was unknown to him.

They reined off the trail, warily watchful and not sure where the bullet had come from. Dust, drifting back from the herd, formed a haze here, and it told Spain that Joe had urged the cattle to a faster gait. He thought, Not too fast, Joe — don't lose them.

Linkervale and his partner had evidently decided upon a strategic move, for now the blocky rider trotted his horse off at an angle, as if intending to circle, while Linkervale remained motionless. Spain fired, the bullet kicking up dust in front of the moving rider and turning him abruptly. The bay shied again, but with less violence; when Spain fired a third time, the animal merely flinched.

Linkervale had him spotted now. The black-bearded rider fired two quick shots that ricocheted off rock nearby, then shouted something to his companion. That one put his horse to a run, heading northward, and Spain understood instantly what they were up to: Linkervale intended to continue the play here while his partner swung around toward the cattle.

Ignoring the circling rider, Spain concentrated on Linkervale. He forced him back into the brush with two bullets that barely missed; then, reloading hastily, Spain mounted the bay and took out after Linkervale, driving him toward his departing partner.

The land here was broken by rock benches festooned with thorny ocotilla and Spanish dagger, while catclaw thickets formed barbed barriers along the dry washes. No rider could strike a straight course; he had to twist and turn, losing time and direction as his horse avoided obstructions. Spain couldn't see Linkervale now, but he heard him clatter noisily across slab rock somewhere to the left. Veering eastward, Spain crossed a wide dry wash and heard hoofbeats directly east. Guessing at once that Linkervale's companion was circling toward the trail, Spain spurred his horse into a reckless, brush-popping charge.

Quartering into the trail, he kept on at top speed for another hundred yards before catching sight of a man's head and shoulders moving fast above brush slightly north and east of him. Spain tilted up the Winchester and took a snap shot without slowing the bay. He saw the man change course, and thought amusedly, You're gun-shy, friend. When he fired again the man doubled back and was soon out of sight. It occurred to Spain now that these Boxed W men weren't any great shakes as gun-fighters. Fists, not bullets, had been Sid Vivian's way of fighting. That realization fashioned a stouter strand of confidence in him, and he thought, Except for Red Gillum, they're probably no better with guns than the homesteaders.

Spain followed a hoof-pocked course along the base of Mesa Parada until he glimpsed Pratt's indistinct shape in trail dust ahead of him; then he angled off into the brush and gave his panting horse a breather. Peering toward a ridge in which a distinct saddle showed, Spain tallied the intervening distance and guessed it to be about three miles, all upgrade and over rock benches. Another hour of travel to reach Big Arroyo and safety.

Spain jacked an empty shell from his Winchester and reloaded; he was wondering what had become of Linkervale when that black-bearded rider came trotting along the trail with a carbine across his left arm. Spain waited until Linkervale passed the thicket, then eased out into the trail and ordered sharply, "Stop right there, Blacky!"

Linkervale stopped, not turning or looking back. He sat rigidly straight in the saddle, the back of his neck glistening, with perspiration. "Don't shoot," he said flatly.

"Let go of the carbine," Spain commanded.

When the weapon fell into the dust, Spain rode up beside Linkervale. Snatching his pistol from its holster, he tossed it aside and asked, "Who's your partner?"

"Name of Umber," Blacky muttered. "What you boys up to?"

"Repossessing some Roman Six cows," Spain said. Giving the land northward a questing gaze, he wondered if Umber were waiting for Linkervale to join him. "Ride ahead of me, at a trot," Spain ordered, and hoped that Umber would dilly-dally long enough for the cattle to reach Big Arroyo.

Umber did. There was no sign of him as Joe Pratt hustled stragglers through the rocky pass. Sam Purdy came down from the south rim to help with the cattle while Spain took up a rear-guard position with his prisoner. When the cattle were all out of the canyon, Spain herded Linkervale up the trail and turned him over to Sam, saying, "Take my friend into camp while I watch for his partner."

"Are we going to keep him a prisoner?" Sam asked, plainly pleased and excited.

Spain nodded, and grinned at Linkervale. "Suits you, doesn't it, Blacky?"

"You galoots must be loco, pulling a stunt like this," Linkervale muttered. "You're asking for bad trouble. But it's no skin off my rump."

Spain ignored that. Eying Sam's sorrel horse, he said, "My pony has covered considerable ground today. How about swapping?"

They were transferring saddles when a remote sound of shooting broke the afternoon stillness. Canting his head to listen, Spain thought, Somebody trying to cross the arroyo. And there was more than one, he reckoned, judging by the continuous reports.

Pulling the latigo snug, Spain got into the saddle. He said, "Step down, Blacky, and turn your pony loose."

"But I'd be afoot," Linkervale protested.

"Do like I say!" Spain snapped, and now, as Blacky obeyed, Spain jabbed the loose horse with his Winchester, shouting, "Vamoose!"

The horse scampered back down the trail into Big Arroyo. Spain said, "Patrol along here until dark, Sam."

"What about Linkervale?"

"Let him walk home," Spain said, and put the sorrel to a run.

Sheriff Ed Kenyon rode into the Cartridge Creek camp shortly after noon wearing double-rigged guns. Ignoring Pat Seely's remark about the extra pistol, Ed accepted a cup of coffee and contemplated the fresh-butchered carcass that hung from a nearby tree. "Where's the hide?" he inquired.

Seely glanced at Ingram, who said soberly, "We toted it out into the brush. Didn't want it drawin' flies."

Kenyon gave a heap of entrails a deliberate appraisal; as if thinking aloud, he mused, "Those guts draw lots of flies."

"Damned if they don't," Ingram agreed.

Finished with his coffee, Kenyon got into the saddle and asked, "Any idea where I might find Clay Spain?"

"Well, he's off toward Big Arroyo," Seely said, "looking for his cows."

"Might be back soon, if you'd care to wait," Ingram said cheerfully.

Kenyon considered that suggestion in

frowning silence for a moment. Then he asked, "You boys realize what you're doing? Do you know how this thing is bound to end up?"

When neither of them spoke, the Sheriff said, "Men with families shouldn't get mixed up in shooting scrapes." He peered at Ingram and asked, "What becomes of Effie and the kids if something happens to you?"

The homesteader studied the scuffed toes of his boots. "Hard to say," he admitted. "Hard to think about, too."

"Well, you'd better think about it," Ed snapped. "You too, Pete. Regardless of the right or wrong of Spain's case, you boys should know better than to jump into something that doesn't concern you."

"Maybe it does concern us," Seely said. "Maybe we've took all we can take from Boxed W."

That seemed to infuriate Ed Kenyon. Temper flared in his faded eyes, and the habitual affability was gone from his voice when he exclaimed, "Lace Fayette has filled you full of bunk!"

"How so?" Ingram asked.

"Why, she's got you all stirred up with her talk. She's got you believing this whole country should be turned into a homesteader's paradise and a big cow outfit has no right in it. Well, that ain't so. You've let Lace Fayette fill your heads with a lot of loco notions. Just because a jury turned Sam Purdy loose is no reason for everybody else to start taking pot shots at Lew Wade's crew."

For a moment the three of them were silent. Then Seely asked, "You think it was all right for Boxed W to grab Spain's cows and rebrand them?"

"I've seen no proof that it was done," Kenyon retorted. "Lew Wade bought some Roman Six cows and has a bill of sale to show he paid for them. If more than he bought were taken, it's up to Spain to prove it in a court of law."

"How could he prove that unless he took the cows?" Ingram asked. "And who could say for sure whether they were the ones Wade bought, or the ones his crew took from Spain?"

Kenyon couldn't answer that, and admitted it with a shrug. But he said stubbornly, "It's no concern of yours, regardless. Clay Spain never did you boys any favors. Why should you feel sorry for him?"

"Maybe we feel sorry for ourselves," Ingram said. "Maybe we want to take a crack at Boxed W any way it can be done."

Kenyon glanced at the hung carcass; he

230

said thoughtfully, "I could arrest you boys on suspicion, and be doing a favor to your families."

"But we wouldn't like it," Ingram warned. "None at all."

Seely nodded agreement to that. "We sure wouldn't."

While Kenyon sat undecided, Seely added, "Our minds are made up on this thing, Ed. We can't be talked out of it. That goes for Pinky Troop and Seth Arbuckle too."

Kenyon shook his head. "You'll regret it," he insisted. "Mind what I'm saying — you'll all regret the day you throwed in with Spain!"

Then he rode out of camp, heading toward Big Arroyo.

CHAPTER NINETEEN

Earl Tipton rode eastward on the rimrock patrol assigned to him until he met Pinky Troop. It was shortly after noon, with the sun obscured by an expanding bank of clouds and a cold wind coming out of the west.

Troop was eating a beef sandwich with apparent relish. "Just like a picnic," he mumbled between bites. "Sure beats followin' a plow."

Earl peered across Big Arroyo, observing how dull and drab the rough brush country appeared without sunlight to give it depth and color. "Any sign of Boxed W riders?" he asked.

"Saw a dust head 'way off yonder some time ago," Pinky said. "You seen anybody?"

Earl shook his head. "Thought I heard some distant gunshots, but I suppose it was just my imagination. Guess I'd better start back."

"No need to be in a hurry," Troop said.

But Earl turned his horse and rode back along the rimrock, keeping an alert watch. He felt better in motion; less apprehensive, somehow. He took out his pipe and tobacco. He thought, There'll be no trouble today. But he couldn't discard the question that had bedeviled him since leaving camp this morning: Could he shoot at another human being? Because he wasn't sure about the answer, a deep sense of foreboding nagged at him. It was an odd thing. He could tell himself that he wasn't afraid of being shot, and believe that this was true. Attempting to analyze his feelings, Earl decided that what he felt wasn't fear. It was dread.

He glanced at the borrowed Winchester in its saddle scabbard. Cap Ledbetter had shown him how to load it and lever out spent shells and how to aim it, using the front and rear sights. But Cap hadn't told him how it was to shoot a man. No one, Earl supposed, could explain that part of it. A fellow had to learn for himself.

Smoking his pipe and keeping a constant watch on Big Arroyo, Earl tried to think about something else, something pleasant — how proud he'd been the day that boy had asked which fist he'd used to give Sid Vivian a bloody nose. And he recalled how it had been with Eve; her frankly eager sharing of his need, her passionate response to his love-making. Earl smiled. Recalling what Clay Spain had told him, he thought, He was right. In his arms Eve hadn't been a cultured, educated lady; she'd been all woman. For the first time in their married life she had become something more than a wife. Something miraculous and exciting. She was his woman.

Earl had crossed the ridge saddle and was topping out beyond it when he glimpsed four riders coming toward Big Arroyo from the north. He thought at once, That was the dust head Pinky saw! In this first moment of discovery his chief reaction was curiosity. Who were they?

Watching them come through the brush, Earl identified Sid Vivian in the lead and Red Gillum behind him. The other two he recognized as Bill Umber and a man named Murdock. They passed behind a rock reef, disappearing one by one, and now the significance of their approach burst upon him: Those four men were intending to cross Big Arroyo!

Hastily dismounting, Earl tied his horse behind a clump of manzanita. His hands shook as he drew the Winchester from its scabbard, and there was a rubbery weakness in his legs when he climbed a rock bench and saw the four riders come into a shallow defile directly across from him.

Earl thought, I've got to stop them!

He felt cold enough to shiver, yet perspiration dripped from his armpits. He cocked the Winchester and aimed it at the trail several yards in front of Vivian. Remembering what Cap had said about pressing a trigger instead of pulling it, he pressed the trigger. The rifle's blast startled him, yet he felt a swift sense of satisfaction at seeing dust spurt up quite close to the spot he had aimed at.

All four riders halted at once. Earl saw Vivian point at him; then, as if executing a plan previously rehearsed, they hastily separated. Vivian whirled his horse off the trail, disappearing behind an upthrust of rock. Gillum galloped down the trail a few yards and turned off into a jumble of huge boulders while the other two backtracked deeper into the defile.

It didn't occur to Earl that they would shoot at him — until a bullet struck the ledge. Rock splinters stung his cheeks, one of them drawing blood. He ducked behind a boulder and heard the vicious *zing* of ricocheting slugs. Yet even then he felt no compulsion to fire at his assailants. His job was to stop them from crossing Big Arroyo.

All those yonder guns seemed to be blasting. Bullets chipped splinters off the boulder on both sides of him. He glanced at his horse, observing the animal's fretful, upheaded reaction to the shooting. "Steady, boy," Earl said, and now, as a slug clipped a branch from the manzanita, he decided to move his horse to a less exposed place. He was easing off the ledge when a bullet struck the horse.

The animal reared back and loosed a piercing whinny as it collapsed. There was a horribly prolonged interval of convulsive threshing. Then the horse's legs went stiff and it lay still.

Shocked and sickened, Earl turned back to the boulder. It seemed fantastic that a bullet could cause such swift destruction. The thought came to Earl that the bullet might have hit him with the same result. If he had reached the horse a few seconds sooner, the bullet would have cut him down. That realization made him wince; and now, for the first time, he was afraid of being shot.

Riding fast, Clay Spain was within a mile of the Big Arroyo saddle when he glimpsed a rider coming from the south. The shooting had subsided to an occasional report.

Had some Boxed W rider circled wide, so as to come in behind Earl? Was that why the firing had decreased?

The possibility caused Spain to leave the rimrock. Angling across successive rock benches, he set a course that would intercept the approaching horseman. He followed a dry wash to the south trail and halted on the fringe of a dense mesquite thicket. The oncoming rider was close enough so that Spain heard his horse's hoof tromp. He had his Winchester cocked and ready when Sheriff Ed Kenyon came trotting around the thicket.

Spain lowered the rifle. He said, "Thought you were somebody else."

Startled, Kenyon demanded harshly, "What's all the shooting about?"

"Difference of opinion, most likely," Spain said, noticing Kenyon's double-rigged guns. "Nothing for you to get mixed up in, Ed."

"You telling me where to ride?"

"No, but this isn't anything you can stop."

Kenyon didn't like that. He scowled and said flatly, "You've got too big for your britches, Clay. You're acting like you own this country."

Spain shrugged, and now he observed an odd thing: Transferring the reins to his right hand, Kenyon brought his left close to the new holster. In that fleeting instant Spain recalled what Earl had told him about the target practice, and he asked sharply, "What's wrong with your right arm, Ed?"

"None of your damned business," Kenyon muttered. He was making up his mind to draw. The intention tightened his eyes and put an increasing pressure on his lips.

"Don't do it," Spain warned. Thumbing back the rifle's hammer, he asked again, "What's wrong with your arm?"

The repetition of that question had a surprising effect. All the cocked tension ran out of Ed Kenyon. His arm dropped and he slumped in the saddle. He looked like a tired old man as he said, "Partial paralysis."

"So that's it," Spain mused, recalling this man's seeming cowardice in the clutch; recalling too what Doc Randall had said when Lace suggested that Ed Kenyon was afraid of Sid Vivian: "It's not that. It's something else."

As if sensing sympathy and not wanting it, Kenyon said stubbornly, "My left hand is all right. All I need is a trifle more practice. And I'm still sheriff, regardless."

"Sure, Ed. Sure you are. But there's no use butting your head against a stone wall." Eager now to have this crippled lawman understand how it was with him, Spain said,

238

"I gave Lew Wade a chance to return those cattle, Ed. I told him what had happened, and why it happened. Vivian hates my guts because I sided Sam Purdy."

"What did Lew say?"

"Well, he as much as admitted that Sid Vivian is the boss. I think Lew is afraid of him."

While Kenyon was absorbing that suggestion, Spain said, "I've got to go see what's happening yonder."

"I'll go have a talk with Lew," Kenyon said, swinging in beside him.

But Spain shook his head. "Not through Big Arroyo, Ed. Angle around to the Boxed W road."

"Why so?" Kenyon demanded.

"Somebody might mistake you for one of us, in which case you'd be shot at."

Kenyon muttered, "A hell of a thing."

"It is for a fact," Spain agreed. He gave Ed a farewell salute and spurred his horse into a run.

A cold wind whipped across the rimrock; it brought the flat crack of sporadic firing as Spain neared Big Arroyo. Peering ahead, he saw Earl Tipton crouched behind a boulder on the crest and glimpsed the movement of his arm as Earl jacked a spent shell from the Winchester. That sight pleased Spain; it proved something that Earl hadn't been sure about himself — his ability to stand under fire.

Spain left his horse in a sheltered crevasse. He was climbing up the rimrock when Earl turned and said, "I'm glad you're here."

His face was pale, so tight and drawn that Spain asked, "You been hit?"

Earl shook his head. "Just sick to my stomach."

Spain eased down beside him. Peering past the boulder, he glimpsed a puff of gunsmoke far up the opposite bank and heard a bullet splatter against nearby rock. Then there was silence.

For upwards of ten minutes there was no more shooting and no sign of movement. Tipton had stopped Boxed W's attempted crossing here. Spain grinned, thinking how odd it was that so inexperienced a warrior should have accomplished so much.

Tipton said gravely, "I had to shoot one of them, Clay. He kept right on coming until I shot him."

"Who was it?"

"I think his name is Murdock." He grimaced. "It was awful. He fell off his horse and tried to get up, but he couldn't. He started crawling back along the trail. I didn't shoot, and after a while Red Gillum came down and got him. Then they began shooting again, but nobody tried to cross."

"You did damned good," Spain said. Understanding how he was feeling, he added, "The first one is always tough, but you'll get over it."

Tipton nodded, and pointed to his dead horse. "That bullet didn't miss me by much, Clay. It made me more afraid than I've ever been."

The confessional tone of his voice made Spain chuckle. He said, "Any man who isn't afraid of a bullet hasn't got good sense." Then he said, "Ride to camp and get yourself another horse while I watch things here."

"You think they'll make another try at crossing?"

"Not till after dark, and we'll be gone by then."

As Tipton went down to the sorrel, Spain called, "Tell those boys in camp to eat an early supper. They'll be standing first guard tonight."

CHAPTER TWENTY

The talk in camp was less jovial than it had been the evening before; voices were subdued and there were long intervals of silence when everyone seemed to be listening. A tarp windbreak had been fashioned against the cold breeze coming off the Barricades, and the fire formed a ruddy island of warmth where men puffed on pipes and cigarettes.

Pinky Troop asked, "You reckon they'll tackle us tonight, Clay?"

Spain shook his head. "Scarcely think so. Vivian probably sent a man for Doc Randall to take care of Murdock. Probably sent another to bring in the line-camp men. That means he's shy three riders tonight."

"You going to try the same game tomorrow?" Sam Purdy asked.

"No, it'll have to be a trifle different." Spain turned to Pratt and said, "Go spell Ingram and Seely for a few minutes. I want them to hear this."

Pratt got up slowly, reluctant to leave the fire. He said, "I must be good, taking the place of two men."

While Joe was saddling his horse, Earl Tipton said moodily, "I hope Murdock doesn't die."

"Murdock would've shot you if he'd got the chance," Troop said, as if wanting Earl to feel better about it.

"And he would've laughed to see you kickin'," Arbuckle said.

There was no need for vengeance in Earl, no spite nor spleen to be vented. Sitting there with his chin cupped in his knee-propped hand, he looked incapable of anger, or vicious intent. Aware of Spain's appraisal, he smiled and said softly, "I was thinking about Eve, and wondering if she misses me."

"You miss her?" Spain asked.

Earl nodded. "Especially at night."

"Then she's probably missing you twice as much," Spain said, and he wondered if Lace Fayette had got back from Tucson. Presently, when Ingram and Seely rode in from the brush, he said, "Here's the setup for tomorrow. Vivian will have his crew watching the flats around West Tank. They'll be all set for another raid. Joe and I will start out early again, but we'll take a different route, along the east side of Cartridge Creek to about ten miles north of Barricades and ride south from there to Calico Seep, which is about seven miles from West Tank. Then we'll cross westward to the Boxed W road ford."

While he paused to pluck a burning twig from the fire and light his cigarette, Arbuckle said, "Sounds like an all-day ride just getting there."

Spain nodded. "We'll camp at the seep tomorrow night. Meanwhile, when we fail to show up on the flats, Vivian will start looking for fresh tracks west of Big Arroyo and won't find any. That'll puzzle him, and Sid doesn't like to be puzzled. By afternoon he'll probably come over here for a look-see. With that idea in mind, I want all six of you to guard the gather and this camp tomorrow."

"How about the next day, when you and Joe start back with the cattle?" Purdy inquired.

"Same setup."

"Will you be coming through the south saddle?"

Spain shook his head. "The long way, north of Boxed W and then down the east side of Cartridge Creek."

There was an interval of silence while the men absorbed the strategy of this plan. Then Pinky Troop exclaimed, "By God, that's neat!"

And Seth Arbuckle bragged, "While them Boxed W bastards cool their heels betwixt West Tank and Big Arroyo, you'll be drivin' off their cattle, pretty as you please!"

Spain glanced at Sam Purdy, saying, "You'll be in charge here. Might be a good idea to set up a circling patrol."

Purdy nodded. "Shouldn't be hard to do with six men." Presently he asked, "Couldn't you use another man, Clay? Five'll be enough here."

Spain thought about it for a moment. Unless Boxed W made an all-out effort, there'd be no need of six men. Finally he said, "Maybe so, Sam," and, looking at Tipton, he asked, "Want to come along with Joe and me?"

"Nothing I'd like better," Earl said.

Afterward, when Pratt came back to the fire, Spain said, "Sleep fast, Joe. We'll be breaking out early in the morning."

Pratt held his hands to the fire. "Probably be raining," he predicted glumly.

It was. A cold, wind-driven rain that felt like sleet. Their slickers were wood-stiff by the time they crossed the creek, where shell ice had formed along the edges.

Traveling by instinct, Spain led the way northward at a slow trot. This, he reasoned, would lessen the chances of discovery, for there'd be no telltale dust signals to reveal their passage across Boxed W range; but it would be a long and tedious day, followed by a misery camp at Calico Seep.

It was still dark when they crossed the muddy ruts of the Boxed W road. An hour later, as the murk thinned to a dismal gray dawn, they forded Cartridge Creek and rode west with the slanting rain full in their faces.

Sometime after noon they climbed into a sheltering band of timber and halted long enough for Earl to make coffee. Afterward, riding west again, they crossed a trail where southbound hoofprints showed. Studying them for a moment, Spain said, "Four riders, sometime last night."

Sid Vivian had pulled in his line-camp men.

The rain eased off late in the afternoon, but low-banked clouds remained, and it was getting dark when they rode into the high-walled pocket where Calico Seep made a muddy smear against the sandstone. Working against time now, they scoured the terrain for wood.

Earl got a fire going and put beef in a skillet. "Won't be so bad if the rain holds off," he said.

The first snowflakes came sifting down while they were eating supper. Joe Pratt peered up. "Snow, by God. Now we're in for it."

But Spain said thoughtfully, "Those flats around West Spring will be white an hour or so from now."

"So'll the cattle," Joe said.

Spain shook his head. "It'll melt on them, because they're warm. But the ground is cold, and so is the brush. Everything will be white except the cattle, and they'll show up real good." He grinned at Tipton, adding, "A new thing for you, Earl. Night roundup."

For upwards of two hours they sat around the campfire, soaking up its heat while melted snow dripped from their hat brims and slickers. There was no wind, but the air got increasingly colder, the snowflakes smaller and drier. Earl, cheerful as always, discussed Lace Fayette's proposed irrigation project. "She may have to postpone it until spring, because of this early winter," he predicted. "But that ditch will be dug. You can bank on that."

Pratt sat in moody silence, sour as a man could be. It occurred to Spain that Joe had changed considerably since his spree in Hondo. Before that he had been easygoing and good-natured, without ambition or regret. Now he brooded most of the time.

"Still feeling bad about Lilybelle?" Spain asked sympathetically.

Pratt nodded.

"Best forget her, Joe."

Pratt's frown deepened. "I'll never forget her. She's the only woman I ever really wanted for keeps." Afterward, as if talking to himself, Joe said, "She thought the same about me for a while. Not with her head, but with her heart. She felt just like I did — like nothing mattered, just so we was together."

"Does she live in Hondo?" Tipton asked.

Joe gawked at him. "You mean you don't know her?"

"Don't believe I do. Where does she live?"

"At Fancy Anne's. The blonde one, with big blue eyes and the nicest shape you ever saw on a female woman."

"You mean — she's a prostitute?" Earl asked.

"What goddamn difference does that make?" Joe demanded. "Just because a woman knows how to handle herself in bed don't keep her from being beautiful, does it?"

That seemed to baffle Tipton. He asked, "But how can a man have respect for a woman who gives herself to other men?"

"She don't. She gets paid for it, which is how most women operate, one way or another. She has to eat, don't she? And buy dresses. What's the difference whether you pay in cash or with groceries and clothes? You're still paying for it, ain't you?"

Spain smiled, watching Tipton attempt to absorb Pratt's philosophy, and thinking it was well that Joe didn't know about Eve's affair with Jack Benteen.

"But a common prostitute —" Earl began.

"She ain't common!" Pratt interrupted. "She's high-class — the best I ever met. And I've saw a hell smear of whores in my time."

That stopped Tipton. He shrugged and smiled. "Every man to his taste."

Presently, as they were saddling the horses, he whispered to Spain, "An odd character, isn't he?"

All that rain-pelted morning five men rode a patient patrol at Cartridge Creek. At noon they began dropping out to eat, one at a time, with Sam Purdy the last to have his warmed-up frijoles and coffee. When he rejoined the patrol, Sam passed the word along to be doubly alert during the remaining hours of daylight. "Vivian will doubtless send somebody to take a look-see. He'll want to know what's going on."

Seth Arbuckle got the warning from Pinky Troop, who remarked, "This weather makes a man wonder what he done with his summer's wages."

Arbuckle nodded in frowning agreement. "Suppose the roof is leaking at home. Alice kept after me to fix it, but I put it off. She'll be fit to be tied."

When Troop rode on, Arbuckle took out his Durham sack. He cursed when water dripped from his down-tilted hat brim, spoiling the cigarette. He dug out a fresh paper and was sifting tobacco into it when Blacky Linkervale eased out of the brush behind him and said sharply, "Don't move!"

Panic gripped Seth Arbuckle. The half-rolled cigarette slipped from his fingers, and the thought flashed through his mind that Linkervale couldn't see the pistol stuck in the front of his slicker. It wasn't more than three inches from his right hand. If he grasped the pistol and whirled —

But now Blacky was riding up behind him. He said, "Hold your hands out where I can see 'em."

Linkervale came up and plucked the pistol from Seth's slicker. He said, "Put your hands behind you," and when Arbuckle obeyed, he tied his wrists securely with a pigging string. Then he uncoiled his rope, dropped a loop over Arbuckle's head, and said, "We're going yonderly."

"Where?"

"Boxed W."

"What for?"

"Sid wants to see you," Linkervale said. Spurring his horse, he warned, "Keep up, or git dragged."

Arbuckle kept up, crowding his horse to keep slack in the rope. Wet brush whipped across his face and snagged his slicker, tearing it. When Linkervale pulled up abruptly, Arbuckle's mount bumped into Blacky's horse, almost upsetting him.

"You goddamn idiot!" Blacky snarled. He hit Arbuckle in the face and commanded, "Watch where you're going!"

"I couldn't help it," Seth whined. "I've got no reins."

There was a rider on the trail ahead of them, coming this way. Linkervale had his gun out. He cocked it and said softly, "If that's one of Spain's bunch, you're a gone gosling."

Arbuckle shivered. Even though he was quite sure it wouldn't be Spain, Tipton, or Pratt, fear knotted in his stomach like a tightening fist. Linkervale meant what he said. Seth could tell that by looking at him. He would shoot and run. Presently Red Gillum rode up through the misty drizzle, and for the first time in his life Seth was glad to see him.

"So you ketched one of them," Red said. "Seen anything of Spain?"

Linkervale shook his head. "I got a good chance at this jigger right off, and grabbed him. Didn't have time to scout the camp."

"I'll go take a look," Gillum said. Riding past, he grinned at Arbuckle. "Your wife'll look real nice in black."

Arbuckle thought about that as he followed Linkervale into Big Arroyo. Crossing the sandy wash, he asked, "What does Sid Vivian want with me?"

"Depends," Linkervale said.

"On what?"

"On Kid Murdock. If he dies, you'll hang."

"But I didn't shoot him," Arbuckle protested. "I wasn't within five miles of this crossing yesterday."

Blacky shrugged. As they climbed the west bank, he said, "Sid don't give a damn who pays for it, just so someone pays. This deal has been too goddamn one-sided. It's got to be evened up."

There were lights at Boxed W, but there was no cheerfulness in them for Seth Arbuckle as he followed Linkervale across the muddy yard. Sid Vivian came to the bunkhouse doorway and asked, "Who you got there?"

"Arbuckle," Blacky reported. "Where you want him put?"

"In the feed room," Vivian said, and went back into the bunkhouse.

Pulling up at the corral fence, Linkervale ordered, "Git down."

"I can't, until you untie my hands," Arbuckle said.

"Oh, yes, you can," Blacky said, and yanked hard on the rope.

Arbuckle tipped out of the saddle. He landed on his back in the mud, bareheaded and gasping for breath.

Linkervale flipped off the loop. He came over and kicked Arbuckle and ordered, "Git up."

Arbuckle obeyed hastily. Then he said, "I dropped my hat."

"You won't be needing no hat," Linkervale muttered. Leading him to the feed room, he pushed Seth inside and locked the door with a harness clasp.

Arbuckle moved against grain sacks and found a place to sit down. The dark room was as cold as a tomb. He shivered so that his teeth chattered, and he had an odd sense of unreality, as if this were a bad dream from which he must awaken. But the aching of his bound arms was real, and so was the fear that gnawed at his stomach.

He hadn't shot Murdock. Or anyone else. Sam Purdy had killed a Boxed W rider, and so had Spain. Earl Tipton had shot Murdock. If someone had to pay, it should be one of them. Not him.

Seth heard the cook call, "Come and get it," and heard men cross the yard to the kitchen. He wondered if Vivian would send him some supper, and didn't much care, for there was no appetite in him.

He heard the crew go back to the bunkhouse. Some time after that there was a remote sound of music — a piano playing part of a tune he didn't know, over and over again. Lew Wade, he thought. A rich man playing his piano while a poor man sat in a cold, dark feed room. At this dismal moment Seth Arbuckle hated all rich, well-fed men, and was so sorry for himself that he felt like crying. What had he ever done to deserve this? Hadn't he always tried to do the right thing, and turned the other cheek so often that he'd been accused of being a coward?

It occurred to him now that Lew Wade might not even know he was being held a prisoner. If he could talk to Lew, perhaps he'd listen to his plea for mercy.

Seth got up and stepped cautiously toward where he thought the door was. He bumped into a feed bin, backed off, and then tripped over some object that caught him across the shins. He fell face down, striking his head against the feed bin. He was trying to get up when the door opened and Sid Vivian stepped inside with a lantern, followed by Red Gillum.

"What you doing — praying?" Red asked derisively.

"Fell down," Arbuckle mumbled, still dazed.

"I'll help you up," Red offered. He grasped a handful of Arbuckle's hair and pulled so hard that Seth yelped.

Vivian stood with the lantern held shoulder-high. He asked, "What's Spain up to?"

"Why, he's after the cows he claims are his," Arbuckle said.

"I mean what's he doing today? There hasn't been a rider cross Big Arroyo."

Arbuckle shrugged. "Spain thought it was too wet for gathering cattle. He decided to just hang on to what we got."

"Where is he now?" Vivian demanded.

"In camp, I suppose."

Vivian shook his head. "Spain hasn't been there all day, and he isn't there now. Red just got back. He says Spain, Tipton, and Pratt are missing."

When Arbuckle didn't answer, Vivian snapped, "Speak up. Where are they?"

"I don't know," Seth muttered.

Vivian's eyes were cold. "You're a goddamn liar."

Arbuckle didn't see Gillum's fist. It came from the side, smashing his cheek with an impact that knocked him against a stack of sacked feed. "Speak up!" Red commanded. "And tell the truth!"

Seth shook his head dazedly. He asked, "How would I know where Spain is?"

"You'd better know," Vivian said. "And you'd better tell me. I've had two men murdered by that bunch, and another bad wounded. I intend to start paying off directly, and you might be number one on the list."

"But I didn't shoot none of your men. Don't take it out on me."

"You're riding with Spain. That's enough. Any man rides with him is a target."

"You going to tell us where Spain is?" Gillum demanded.

Seth wanted to tell them. He wanted to end this nightmare, here and now. But some fragile strand of loyalty held him back. If he told where Spain was, there'd be an ambush. It would be the end of Spain and Tipton and Pratt, and the end of any fight against Boxed W, too.

Gillum took out his jackknife and opened it. He asked, "Which ear you want first, Sid?"

"The right one," Vivian said flatly.

"You can't do that to me!" Arbuckle blurted. "It ain't human!"

But Red reached for Seth's ear with his left hand, and when Seth dodged, Red warned, "Stand still, or you might lose half your face."

Then, grasping the tip of the ear tightly, Gillura slashed off the upper half with deft swiftness while Seth tried to duck away. Tossing it toward Vivian, Gillum said amusedly, "Now the left one."

"No!" Arbuckle screamed. Backing to a corner, he whimpered, "I'll tell you where they are."

CHAPTER TWENTY-ONE

It had stopped snowing when they reached West Tank, shortly before nine o'clock. They found sixteen cows with calves near the windmill, their dark shapes plainly visible against the white ground. Spain said, "We'll use this for our holdup," and led on into the snow-frosted brush beyond the tank.

This night gather, he thought, would give them several hours' head start. By daylight they should be far north of Boxed W, and they should cross Cartridge Creek before noon. Riding past small groups of cows, he told his companions, "We'll get a good bunch off these flats tonight."

For three hours then they worked the country around West Tank, pushing cattle toward the windmill. It was slow, cold, tedious work, the horses sliding and slipping when forced to turn sharply. When Spain took a rough tally of the gather, he estimated there were over sixty cows, with nearly as many calves. Enough to handle on a night drive. It took a little time to get the herd lined out and moving northward, but once that was accomplished, the cattle plodded along like the seasoned trail brutes they were.

Spain rode the east flank of the driven herd, shifting back and forth from point to drag, while Earl Tipton did likewise on the west side, with Joe Pratt hustling the drags. Spain felt highly optimistic. With this bunch added to yesterday's gather, the job would be half done; a few more raids and it would be finished. It would be a fine thing to ride into Hondo and tell Lace the Roman Six cows had been repossessed; to hold her in his arms and collect his reward. Recalling how it had been, with Lace receptive but not responsive, he thought, She'll warm up when the time comes. With proper handling, Lace would discard her habitual reserve, and once she did that she'd be a woman worth waiting for.

Just thinking about her made the night seem less cold. When all this was over he'd spend some cozy evenings in town with Lace. Some nights, too. It occurred to him that he might not want to sell his share of the Roman Six cows; that there was plenty of range in this country if a man wanted to settle down. Once the raids were finished, there shouldn't be too much trouble with Boxed W. No more than a man would find anywhere. Remembering what Gail Purdy had said about trouble, Spain understood that she was right. A man couldn't run away from trouble, no matter how far he rode.

They were crossing a brushless slope northwest of Boxed W when Spain noticed horse tracks in the snow. Dismounting at once, he lit a match and studied them, observing that seven or eight riders had passed here so recently that the shoe marks showed no blur at all. And they were headed directly toward Calico Seep.

That discovery shocked Clay Spain. Why should the Boxed W crew ride toward Calico Seep at this time of night?

What possible reason could there be for such a trip — unless Vivian knew that three men planned to camp there?

But how could Vivian have known that?

Abruptly then the answer came to Spain. Someone had told his plans to Vivian. And hard on the heels of that understanding came the rest of it. Dropping back to where Joe Pratt rode, Spain said, "Vivian must've raided the Cartridge Creek camp and made somebody talk. He's on his way to Calico Seep with the whole crew, right now."

"No!" Pratt exclaimed. "By God, we're in for it!"

Spain nodded. "They'll trail us to West Tank, and then over here."

"What we going to do?"

Thinking this out as he went along, Spain said, "If they overtake us this side of the timber we're licked. And if we make it into the woods they can bottle us up there till we starve to death. Three men can't fight and drive cattle at the same time."

"Why don't we just take off for camp, and to hell with the cattle?" Joe suggested.

Spain thought about that for a moment. Then he said, "There's one way we might make it — just one way."

"How's that?" Joe asked.

But Spain was already spurring his horse up the west side of the herd toward Earl Tipton.

Lew Wade poured himself a cup of tea at the kitchen table. The crew had ridden out hours ago on what Sid Vivian referred to as a finish fight with Clay Spain. Recalling Sid's confident declaration, Lew grimaced. He could imagine what would happen, with men shooting at one another and leaving bloodstains on the snow. Violence was distasteful to Lew Wade at any time, and it

261

seemed fantastic that men should battle so soon after Kid Murdock had been taken to town with a bullet in his groin. Sid and the crew had heard Murdock groan piteously as they loaded him into the wagon, yet now they were out exposing themselves to more bullets. There had been too much fighting these past weeks. Too much bloodshed. Sid had gone berserk since Lin Graham's death.

Wade took a sip of hot tea and contemplated the sheet of music propped against the sugar bowl. These first few measures of "Midnight Lace" had come so easily, with such little effort. Lew smiled, thinking how inspired he had been, how pleased and proud. There was good music in those measures. The notes had a fine rhythmic flow. There was a sense of nostalgia in them; a bittersweet flavor of remembering and wanting, of lack and loneliness. But the measure he was working on now didn't seem inspired at all. It needed something. And the tempo wasn't right.

He paid no heed to the sound of hoofs in the yard. The crew had come back, he supposed, and he hoped none of the men were wounded. He was taking another sip of tea when the door opened and Clay Spain stepped inside with a cocked gun in his hand.

Wade stared at him in astonishment. "What are you doing here?" he asked.

"Put on your hat and coat," Spain ordered. "You're going for a ride."

"But why should I ride with you?"

"Because I say so," Spain muttered. He stepped over to the table and waggled the gun menacingly close to Wade's head. "Get moving right now or I'll bust you," he warned.

Wade moved, and now, as the Chinese cook came from his bedroom, Spain said, "You tell Sid Vivian that I've taken Mr. Wade with me. Tell him Lew will be a target if there's any shooting. You understand?"

The frightened cook nodded. He hugged his nightshirt closer to his chest and watched Wade put on a pair of gloves. "You come back soon, Mista Lew?"

"Soon as possible, Charlie," Wade said. When they went outside, he peered at the moving cattle and demanded, "What are those cows doing in this yard?"

"Just passing through, is all," Spain said, and prodded him toward the corral.

Presently, as Wade saddled himself a horse, Spain said, "We'll ride drag, and don't you try to leave it."

"But what's this all about?" Wade demanded.

263

"I'll tell you tomorrow, if we're both alive then," Spain said. As they caught up with the drag, he added amusedly, "Bet this is the first time you've done any trail-herding at night."

"It is," Lew agreed. "In fact, it's the first I've ever done, day or night." And while Spain was absorbing that news, Wade added morosely, "I detest cattle."

Spain belabored the rumps of laggard cows with a rope end. He shouted, "Go on, cattle — go on!"

Halting occasionally to listen for sounds of pursuit, Spain wondered about this man that rode with him so reluctantly. Lew Wade had never appeared to be a cowman, and now he admitted he didn't like cattle, yet he owned the biggest ranch in Apache Basin.

"If you detest cattle, why are you in the business?" Spain asked.

"I've never had any choice," Lew explained. "Inherited Boxed W from my father. He always resented the fact that I wanted to be a musician, so he wrote into the will that the ranch would belong to me only if I lived on it. Otherwise it would go to his brother in Kansas."

"So?" Spain mused, and pushed the drags until they were tromping on the heels of those ahead. "Seems odd that a man brought up on a ranch wouldn't like cow work."

"Perhaps it is odd," Lew admitted. "But I've always detested violence in all its forms. I can't stand the sight of blood. Seeing a calf castrated makes me sick to my stomach. That's why I have an understanding with Sid Vivian. He runs the ranch and gets fifty per cent of the profit as salary. It makes a good arrangement for both of us. He does the dirty work, and I do what I've always wanted to do — write music."

Spain chuckled, understanding now many things that had puzzled him. No wonder Lew appeared to be afraid of his foreman, or that Sid acted as if he owned Boxed W. In all of Cattleland there'd never been a setup like this: a cowman who preferred music to cattle, and a ramrod who got half the profits in wages.

When the herd plodded into a rock-bordered trail that led to Big Arroyo, Spain called Joe Pratt back to the drag. "Keep an eye on Wade," he said.

"You hear 'em coming?" Joe asked.

Spain shook his head. "I'm going to stay back a ways, just in case."

Turning off the trail, he put his horse up a steep embankment, pulled in behind a rock reef, and dismounted. Vivian should have overtaken them by now, unless he had decided against it because of Wade. There had been plenty of time. Spain canted his head, listening for sounds of travel and hearing none. A snowflake touched his cheek, then another and another. It began snowing hard; large, wet flakes, falling so thickly that the night seemed darker now. And colder. Spain stomped his feet, and wondered what time it was. Must be midnight or after. A long day asaddle. But the worst of it would be over when the cattle were across the Big Arroyo.

Thinking how near to failure this night raid had come, Spain grinned. Kidnaping Wade was the only thing that could have kept Boxed W's crew from breaking up the trail drive. Thinking about it now, Spain marveled that his scheme had worked so well. Even though Vivian wouldn't want to risk shooting his employer and losing what amounted to a half interest in Boxed W, it seemed odd that Sid wouldn't make an attempt to scatter the herd. Sid should have guessed that Wade would be riding with the drags; taking that for granted, he could have done his shooting at the point.

Abruptly then Spain thought, Maybe that's what he's doing now — swinging around to the front end!

With that suspicion building swiftly in him, Spain mounted at once. Riding down to the trail, he halted for a moment, listening, and considering which side of the herd Vivian would choose for a flanking movement. There was no way of knowing, but he remembered that a long dry wash paralleled this trail a quarter mile or so to the south. He angled southeastward through breeze-slanted snowflakes that pelted his right cheek. Visibility was so poor now that he didn't see the wash until his pony began following the sandy course. Spain dismounted and, crouching, struck a match. It went out almost instantly, but not before he had glimpsed fresh hoofprints.

Spain cursed and climbed hastily into the saddle. There was no doubt about it now. Vivian intended to stop the herd this side of Big Arroyo. Urging his horse to a trot, Spain put his mind to guessing where the blockade would occur. West of the saddle there were a dozen likely spots. Tautly listening as he rode, Spain peered through a slanting screen of snow. The wind was out of the west and at his back now. He thought, They'll hear me before I can see them, and cocked his Winchester.

Presently dismounting again, Spain used three matches before discovering the tracks, which were already filling with snow. When he rode on the snow came against his left cheek, which told him that the wash had turned northward toward the trail. Dredging up a mental picture of the land here, he recalled that the wash bent away from the arroyo's saddle less than a mile from the rim. The blockade spot must be near.

Moments later a vague pink stain appeared ahead of him and a trifle to the north. For a moment, as his horse trotted on along the wash, Spain couldn't identify what he'd glimpsed. Blinking his eyes, he peered at an odd recurring alteration in the gray curtain of slanting snow. It was weird, like a faint reflection of moonlight against clouds. Pink moonlight. Then he realized that it must be firelight reflected on falling snow, and understood why it was there. Sid Vivian was using a fire to blockade the trail!

His first impulse was to swing around and attack the bunch at the fire; to drive them off the trail. It seemed monstrous that this raid, so near success, should be ruined now. But even if he managed to force Vivian's crew out of the trail, the bonfire would be an effective barrier, and their bullets would scatter the herd. Halting now, Spain wondered if he had time to reach the cows and turn them southward into this wash. If that could be accomplished, there might be a chance of bypassing the fire and the men waiting there. The sound of their passing wouldn't carry far in this storm.

Spain turned back, quartering toward the trail and crossing a rocky ridge to reach it. Glancing back, he saw no sign of the bonfire now. Vivian, he guessed, had been smart enough to build it on a bend of the trail where intervening brush and boulders would obscure the flames until the lead cows were close to them.

Spain was facing directly into the storm now. The wind-driven snow smothered the sound of his pony's hoofbeats and closed out everything beyond a few yards away. When he wiped snow from his face, the sleeve of his slicker cracked like a breaking board. He rubbed his cheeks; feeling them burn, he wondered if they were frostbitten.

Spain's pony threw up its head, ears pointing forward. A moment later Spain observed a vague form coming toward him, and wondered why Earl was riding in front of the cattle. He was on the verge of calling Earl's name when the oncoming rider announced, "They're a couple of miles back."

Red Gillum's voice.

Coming close now, Gillum asked, "That you, Umber?"

269

"Yeah," Spain muttered, and thumbed back the Winchester's hammer.

Gillum leaned forward in the saddle. "Spain!" he blurted, and the barrel of his arm-cradled rifle swung around.

Spain fired twice at this point-blank range, and saw Gillum tip over as his horse shied sideways across the trail. Feeling no pity, he watched Red Gillum fall headlong into the snow and die. This meeting, Spain thought, had been in the cards since the night Gillum kicked in his ribs. He rode around the body and tried to grasp the riderless pony's reins, but the animal shied away. Yanking his horse in a pivoting turn, Spain hazed Red's mount off the trail and hoped it would go to the ranch, rather than to the bonfire.

Riding on, he thought about the abrupt ending of his long feud with Red Gillum. It had been inevitable that one of them should die; only the time and the place had been undecided. Now it was finished, and Spain blessed his luck. Red, he supposed, had been sent to find out how near the oncoming herd was. Without his warning to alert them, that Boxed W crew might warm their shanks at the fire for a considerable time before sensing that something was wrong.

The lead cows were like frosty apparitions

protruding from a ghostly screen. Spain blocked the trail, shouting at them and turning them southward. When Tipton came up, slumped in the saddle and seemingly half asleep, Spain said, "Vivian's crew is up ahead. We'll use the wash to get around them."

"What wash?" Earl asked stupidly.

Spain poked him. "Wake up or you'll freeze to death," he warned. "Move your arms and legs."

Tipton shook himself, his slicker crackling. "You say the Boxed W crew is ahead of us?"

"Yes, and we've got to angle around them to reach Big Arroyo. You stay here and turn the cattle until Joe comes up. Tell him the news and then work the south side of the herd toward the front."

Spurring his tired pony back and forth along the line of plodding cattle, Spain kept the herd from disintegrating between trail and wash, and kept watching and listening for approaching riders. Sid Vivian wouldn't remain idle long. Wondering why Gillum didn't return, he would investigate. Just a matter of time, Spain thought, and took comfort in the belief that the lead cows in this herd were already past the blockade.

Sid Vivian stood at the bonfire with Blacky

Linkervale while Bill Umber and three line-camp men gathered wood. He muttered, "What's keeping Red so long?"

"Them cows must've been farther back than we supposed," Blacky said. "Bad night to travel."

A rider dragged a dead mesquite tree up to the fire, disengaged his rope, and held his hands to the flames. "Gittin' colder," he remarked.

Vivian kept peering westward into the slanting snow. "This is what comes of Ed Kenyon's refusing to arrest Spain," he muttered. "A ranch owner ain't safe in his own home with that bastard running loose. If he harms Lew —"

Sid stopped speaking as Bill Umber raced up and shouted, "Red is back there in the trail — dead!"

"Dead?" Vivian echoed.

Umber nodded. "Shot twice through the chest."

Vivian cursed and turned to his horse. "Another good man gone!" he raged. "Never saw such goddamn luck as we're having!" Then he asked, "How about the cattle?"

"Didn't see 'em," Umber said, "but I heard somethin' south, toward that dry wash."

Vivian climbed into the saddle. "Mount up, mount up!" he commanded. "Kiley — Swede — come in!" he shouted. "Kiley! Swede!"

Impatiently waiting for the men, he warned, "Be damned sure you don't shoot Lew. Bust the herd, but watch out for Lew."

CHAPTER TWENTY-TWO

The wind was stronger now. It lashed the dry wash with a howling violence that kicked up great swirls of surface snow and flung it into swift-forming drifts. The lead cows kept stopping to wait for tired calves; confused by blinding sheets of snow, they milled about, holding up those behind. Spain was in the midst of them, cursing and swinging a rope end, when he heard a remote disturbance in back of him. While he listened he caught wind-borne fragments of shrill voices and then the muffled blasting of guns.

He thought instantly, They've jumped us! and spurred his pony to a lope. Swerving around the snow-blurred shapes of cows, he cursed the cattle that got in his way and the pelting snow that half blinded him. Dully, as a man sensing defeat but not accepting it, he realized that the herd was already broken up — that no power on earth could keep the cows from scattering now. When a vague form loomed up ahead of him, Spain held his fire, fearing it might be Tipton or Pratt. The rider yelled at the cattle; he was driving a bunch across the wash and up its south bank when Spain fired. As the rider disappeared, another came off the north side of the wash. This one yelled, "That you, Bill?"

"No, by God!" Spain shouted, and slammed a shot at him and charged head on.

The rider fired and wheeled sharply away. Spain didn't hear the bullet strike, but he felt his pony miss stride. In the next instant, as Spain kicked free of the stirrups, the gelding went down.

Spain landed on his left shoulder. He was attempting to roll free of the threshing pony when a hoof struck him on the right temple. Shock ran through him in one numbing wave. For a queerly blank interval he had no understanding of what had happened to him, no sense of sight or sound or feeling. Afterward he became aware of an indefinite thudding ache. Slowly then his senses returned and he understood that he had to get up; that unless he did so soon, he would freeze to death.

Spain got to his hands and knees. The

movement set up a pounding ache that made him sick to his stomach. He lifted a hand to his temple and felt a crust of frozen blood. The dead horse, sprawled so near he could have touched it, was coated with snow. It occurred to Spain now that he had dropped his Winchester. He was peering about for it when a remote sound of voices came downwind to him. Dropping on his side, Spain tried to unbutton his frozen slicker so that he could get at his pistol. But his cold-stiffened fingers didn't function properly, and so he lay unmoving as two indistinct shapes came into the wash not more than ten feet west of him.

Spain caught fragments of talk. He heard Sid Vivian say, "We've got to find him."

Spain wondered if he was the one they were seeking, and doubted it. More likely Vivian was hunting Lew Wade. But there was no doubt in his mind as to what would happen if Vivian discovered him now. Spain got the slicker unbuttoned; he was calculating the risk of opening it enough to reach his pistol when the two riders went on across the wash.

Luck, Spain thought. Getting back to his knees, he searched for the Winchester and soon found it. When he stood up his legs were like wooden stilts. He stamped his feet.

Relieved at the prickling sensation that came into them, he wriggled his toes and sighed thankfully, "They're not frozen!"

Seth Arbuckle rode into the Cartridge Creek camp shortly after nine o'clock. Challenged by Sam Purdy, who was standing guard, Seth announced, "It's me, Sam — and I'm quitting this outfit."

When they got to the fire Seth showed him his mutilated ear. "They threatened to hang me," he explained. "They made me tell where Clay Spain was."

Pinky Troop got out of his bedroll. "Who did that to you?" he demanded.

"Red Gillum, with Vivian watching," Arbuckle said. He shivered, remembering it. "First they were going to hang me. But Vivian wanted to know where Spain was. Red cut off my right ear and was going to cut the other one."

Bert Ingram asked, "Did you tell them?"

Arbuckle nodded. "I couldn't stand bein' cut on again." He glanced at Pete Seely and asked, "Wouldn't you of done the same?"

"Well, I don't rightly know," Pete said thoughtfully. "Tellin' a thing like that would go agin the grain. But so would havin' my ears cut off."

Arbuckle held a palm over the blood-crusted remnant of his ear. He said, "It hurts awful. I got to go see Doc Randall."

"Did Sid's crew start for Calico Seep?" Purdy asked.

Arbuckle nodded. "They turned me loose and said I'd be shot on sight next time they saw me west of the Horseshoe Hills."

"Those bastards will massacre Spain and Tipton and Pratt," Troop said. "They'll be wiped out with no chance at all."

"How long ago did the crew leave Boxed W?" Purdy asked.

"Must've been better'n an hour ago. Maybe two."

As if guessing what Sam had in mind, Troop said morosely, "We couldn't get there in time to do no good. It's done by now."

Arbuckle got into his saddle. He said, "We're licked and we might as well admit it. Even if this hadn't happened, we couldn't of got Spain's cows out in this kind of weather. It's turnin' into a regular damned blizzard."

They all gazed at him in reflective silence. It was a silence that seemed more accusing than words to Seth Arbuckle. "By God, you can't blame me!" he insisted. "I couldn't just stand there and let Red Gillum cut on me!" Then he said again, "I've got to go see Doc Randall," and rode out.

Presently, as they heard his horse shatter shell ice at the creek, Pinky Troop said, "A man can't be blamed for being what he is."

Hard-driven snow spattered against the tarp windbreak; it slanted over the canvas and formed fleecy coatings on the opened bedrolls. Out in the brush a cow bellowed forlornly for a lost calf.

Pete Seely busied himself making a pot of coffee. Afterward, while they squatted around the fire and drank hot coffee, Bert Ingram looked at Sam and asked, "What'll we do?"

Sam peered into the glowing coals for a long moment as if seeking some answer there. Finally he said, "I don't know, Bert. I just don't know."

Later, when the others got back into their blankets, Sam remained at the fire. He was still sitting there when Earl Tipton rode in and said urgently, "Open up Joe Pratt's bedroll. He's been shot!"

Sam jumped to his feet. "Is Spain with him?"

Tipton shook his head. "Lew Wade. We couldn't find Clay."

Plodding through ankle-deep snow toward Big Arroyo, Clay Spain wondered how Tipton and Pratt had fared. The herd, he supposed, was scattered every which way. He cursed, thinking how close they had come to bypassing Vivian's blockade. Gathering those cows and calves again would be a tedious chore in this kind of weather; a chore that might take days to accomplish. He stumbled over a snow-shrouded boulder and fell headlong. Soon after that he walked into a mesquite thicket and understood that he had wandered out of the wash. Confused now, he tried to get his bearings, and decided he was traveling too far east — that he should head south in order to reach Big Arroyo.

When he went down again he had an impulse to lie there and rest for a while. The cushioning snow gave him an odd sense of protective warmth; it brought a comforting drowsiness. But Spain shook his head and thought, I've got to get up.

He had lost all track of time when he found himself slipping and sliding down the trail into Big Arroyo. His legs ached and his feet were sore in the frozen boots. So near exhaustion now that he could scarcely stand, Spain propped himself against the lee side of a huge boulder. There was scarcely any wind here at the bottom, but he reckoned the snow would be deeper up on the east side of the arroyo.

"I need a fire," he told himself.

It took him five minutes to work up ambition enough to stumble around and grope for a thicket where he could collect dead twigs. When he finally got a blaze going, he used its light to gather wood. With a good fire crackling, he took off his damp gloves and held his palms to the flames. He soaked up the heat. Relaxed now, he was aware of hunger and the need for a smoke. And by these tokens he understood that he was all right. There had been a bad time back there when the only thing he wanted was to lie down, but he was all right now.

Spain shaped up a cigarette and smoked it and listened to the wind's steady blowing above him. This was the earliest snowstorm he could remember in Apache Basin, and about the hardest he'd ever seen. It beat hell that this should have to happen at a time when he was making a tough roundup.

Sitting now with his back against the boulder and his boots to the fire, Spain wondered if Vivian would come into Big Arroyo searching for Wade. He plucked a shell from his gun belt and shoved it into the Winchester's loading chamber and said flatly, "I hope he does."

Shooting Red Gillum, he knew, hadn't settled anything. Sid Vivian was the fountainhead of all this trouble; his was the vicious, unbending will that ruled Boxed W and thus the rest of Apache Basin. Not Lew Wade, as most folks thought. And nothing less than a well-aimed bullet would ever change that will to rule or ruin.

Spain was thinking about that, and knowing instinctively that only one of them would survive this war, he or Vivian, when he observed two riders coming toward him from the east trail. Stepping hastily away from the fire, he stood at the boulder's edge, Winchester raised and ready for firing.

When they were within fifty feet of him, Spain called, "Who's out there?"

They halted, and now one man called, "Is that you, Clay?"

Spain lowered the gun. He stepped out into the firelight and called cheerfully, "Come up and warm yourself, Sam."

When Purdy and Troop dismounted, Spain grinned and said, "Glad to see you boys. I'm afoot."

Sam told him about Joe Pratt. "We sent him to my place in the chuck wagon with Lew Wade while Bert goes on ahead to get Doc Randall. Gail will take good care of Joe until Doc gets there."

"Is he hurt bad?" Spain asked.

"Pretty bad," Sam said. "In the chest."

That news hugely depressed Spain. Climbing up behind Sam for the ride to camp, he said, "Poor Joe's luck has been bad ever since we left Sonora."

While they halted to rest the horses part way up the east bank, Sam told him about Arbuckle. "Seth felt awful about it, Clay. But I guess he just couldn't stand being cut on."

"Red won't use his knife on anybody else," Spain muttered.

When they rode into camp at daylight Pete Seely and Earl Tipton greeted Spain with frank delight. "By grab, we thought you was a goner for sure!" Pete exclaimed.

Earl shook hands, so filled with emotion that he could scarcely speak at all. "Clay," he said. "Clay — I'm glad!"

Pete got busy at the chuckbox, which had been taken off the wagon. "I'll have some grub for you in a jiffy," he promised.

"Do you think there's any chance they'll jump us this time of day?" Sam Purdy asked.

Spain nodded. "From now on, any time at all."

CHAPTER TWENTY-THREE

Spain was asleep in his bedroll when Bert Ingram drove the wagon into camp. The racket roused him and he sat up, blinking sleep-swollen eyes and observing that scarcely any snow was falling.

Ingram tooled the wagon up close to the fire. He peered at Spain and exclaimed, "Thought you was dead!"

"No," Spain said stupidly, still half asleep. "Just getting some shut-eye, is all."

Bert got down and unhooked the trace chains. "I told 'em in town that you was missing, and most likely dead. Lace Fayette felt awful bad about it. So did Cap Ledbetter. He said you put him in mind of Jeb Stuart. When I stopped by at Sam's place to pick up the wagon, his sister acted all broke up about you being gone."

"Gone, hell," Spain said. He stretched and yawned. Fully awake now, he asked, "How's Joe Pratt?"

"Doc Randall says he hasn't got a chance. Just a matter of time."

"How much time?"

"Tonight or tomorrow. Joe's out of his head half the time. Keeps yelling for that dame Lilybelle. He don't say nothing about hurting. All he talks about is Lilybelle. It was so pitiful I rode all the way back to town and ask her to come see him. But she just laughed at me."

Spain cursed. Pulling on his boots, he muttered, "She could do that much for Joe. She could hold his hand while he dies."

"Sure, but you know how them sporty dames are. All they want is a man's money."

Spain went over to the fire and poured himself a cup of coffee. He glimpsed Pinky Troop riding circle out in the brush, and presently saw Earl cross an opening farther north. The held cattle, he supposed, had drifted during the storm last night. One thing, though, they'd drift east, which was the right direction for them to go.

When Ingram joined him at the fire, Spain asked, "What time is it?"

"Must be three-thirty or four. Soon be dark."

Presently Spain went to an upended saddle and picked up a bridle. This, he supposed, was Joe Pratt's gear. "Tell Sam I've gone to town on an important errand," he said.

Ingram squinted at him. "You going to ask Lilybelle to call on Joe Pratt?"

"No," Spain said. "I'm going to tell her to."

The snow was fetlock deep in most places. It had been blown into occasional drifts, with bare ground where the wind had got in its best licks. Some of the cattle had crossed Cartridge Creek and were foraging in thickets on the other side; the flats were tromped into a vast pattern of diverging criss-crossing trails.

There was scarcely any wind now. The air was bitter cold, and Spain thought, There'll be a real freeze tonight. By dark his nose and ears were tingling; he rubbed them occasionally and was glad when he saw the lamplit windows of Sam Purdy's place.

Lew Wade met him at the door. "Why, Clay!" Lew exclaimed. "They told me you were dead!"

The ranch owner seemed genuinely pleased, and that baffled Spain. Lew showed no resentment for having been forced to leave his ranch last night. "What are you doing here?" Spain asked.

"Why, making myself useful," Lew said.

"Miss Gail has her hands full with Joe Pratt. There's chores to do, you know."

Gail came from Sam's bedroom then. She peered at Spain in wide-eyed astonishment. "Clay! You're all right?"

"Sure," Spain said, and took off his hat. "How's Joe?"

"Not very good. But he's awake now, if you'd like to see him." She looked at the fresh scar on Spain's temple and asked, "What happened to you?"

"Got kicked by a dying pony," Spain said, and went into the bedroom, where Joe Pratt lay propped against two pillows.

The little man was staring straight ahead, and his eyes seemed large and dark against the pallor of his face.

"Hello, Joe."

Pratt looked at him without any change of expression.

"How you feel, Joe?"

"Bad. Tol'able bad."

"I'm sure sorry you got hurt," Spain said. "Sorry as hell."

That didn't seem to register at all. Pratt peered straight ahead again. Presently he said, "I been thinkin' about a lot of things, lyin' here. About Sonora and that big pooler outfit we started."

Spain was vaguely aware of Gail and Wade

talking quietly in the kitchen. He thought, They've been keeping a death watch on Joe. Now, for a little bit, they're free of it. It was a tough chore, waiting for a man to die. And Joe was dying. You could see it in his eyes.

"We had us some great old times in Sonora," Joe said. But there was no sign of pleasure in his shrunken face or in his flat-toned voice.

Presently he asked, "Remember that swivel-rumped dancer in El Tanque — the one Dan Tennant and Gus Jubal fought over so hard?"

"Yes, Joe. I remember her."

Joe coughed, sounding like a croupy child. He lifted a limp, seemingly bloodless hand and wiped red-flecked spittle from his lips. "She could sure dance real good," he reflected. "She was a looker."

For a long moment he seemed content to lie there remembering the El Tanque dancer. Then he said, "But she couldn't compare with Lilybelle."

Now, for the first time since entering the room, Spain saw a pleased expression alter Joe's sallow face. A wistful, bittersweet smile slanted his pale cheeks as he said, "I had a dream about her last night. About Lilybelle. I thought she was rubbing my forehead with a nice cool cloth. But when I woke up it was Sam Purdy's sister."

Soberly now, like a small boy voicing an unattainable and fabulous wish, Joe said, "I'd sure like to see Lilybelle one more time."

A lump came into Clay Spain's throat. Here, he thought, was another one like Dan Tennant; another man thinking about a woman while he died.

"Maybe you will," Spain said. "Maybe you'll see her tonight."

Pratt peered at him, his eyes intently questioning. "You really think so, Clay?"

Spain nodded. Strongly aware of Joe's fever-bright eyes, he explained, "She'd of been here by now except for the big snowstorm. But she'll come."

"You sure, Clay? You positive?"

Spain nodded, and now, as Gail came in with a bowl of steaming broth, he said, "I'll go do the chores."

"Take a look at the trail and see if you see her coming," Joe said eagerly.

Crossing the kitchen, Spain observed that the table was set with three places. He said to Wade, "Tell Gail I'll be back about nine o'clock with Lilybelle."

Hondo seemed different with snow on the ground. Long icicles, hanging like tinseled trimmings from the eaves of the Hondo Bank, shone multicolored above the lamplit windows of Lace's second-story living quarters. Glancing up at those windows, Spain had a strong impulse to stop and see Lace, to bask for a brief time in the warmth and fragrance of her presence. That's what a man needed on a cold night like this. A woman's arms around him. A cozy room with the lamp turned low. Just enough light to see how sweet and tantalizing she was; to see her moist, parted lips. But there was no time to spare. If Joe Pratt were to see his beloved Lilybelle, it would have to be soon. Very soon.

Spain rode into Shiloh Alley, glanced at Fancy Anne's place as he passed, and went on to Ledbetter's Livery. This chore shouldn't take long, if Cap would co-operate.

Cap would, gladly. A team of matched bays was being harnessed by the time Spain entered Fancy Anne's parlor.

The red-haired madam greeted him with professional good humor. "They were wrong about you, weren't they, Mr. Spain? Have you any preference between blonde and brunette?"

"Blonde," Spain said.

Fancy Anne went out to the stair well,

called, "Lilybelle!" and went on back to the kitchen.

Spain stepped over to the front window and saw that the team had been hitched to a two-seater carriage.

Lilybelle came into the parlor garbed in a blue silk kimono, black net stockings, and high-heeled gold slippers. Spain thought instantly that she was no prettier than a hundred other blonde trollops he had seen, her lace-sheathed breasts no higher, her legs no more shapely. In this moment while she smiled at him Spain wondered why Joe Pratt had been so hugely impressed by such an ordinary package.

"Hello, handsome," she said. "Is it cold outside?"

Spain nodded, and heard the carriage pull up in front. Then he said, "Joe Pratt is dying. He wants to see you."

The smile faded from Lilybelle's lips. "My goodness, how many times do I have to tell you fellows that I'm not interested in Joe Pratt? He was just a customer who spent a few dollars with me. Why should I put myself out to go see him?"

"Because he loves you," Spain said. "Or thinks he does."

That amused Lilybelle. Hands on hips, she laughed at him. "Love!" she scoffed.

"Why, that little pip-squeak is just a dollar bill with ears to me."

"You trollop!" Spain muttered, and grabbed her. When she opened her mouth to scream, he slapped her face. "Shut up, or I'll bust you good!"

Propelling her to the door, he opened it, and heard a bell tinkle out back. He thought, No time to lose. Picking her up, he ran out to the carriage.

"You can't do this!" Lilybelle protested as he put her in the rear seat. "I'll have you arrested!"

Cap Ledbetter handed over a blanket and a lap robe, and now, as Spain tucked them around his squirming passenger, Fancy Anne called from the front stoop, "Lilybelle, you'll catch your death of cold!"

Ledbetter trotted the horses out of Shiloh Alley, then whipped them into a run. The two horses in front, and Spain's horse tied behind, made a terrific clatter on Main Street's frozen ruts. A man poked his head out of the hotel doorway and yelled, "Where's the fire?"

"You can't do this!" Lilybelle cried. "You can't!"

Ignoring her, Spain said to Cap, "There's a drift half a mile beyond the cattle pens."

Cap eased down and had his team pulling

squarely when they came to it. In the middle, where snow was hub-deep and the wagon stalled momentarily, Lilybelle made a desperate attempt to escape, but Spain hauled her back. He clamped her close to him with one arm and fixed the blanket about her with the other. "Want to catch your death of cold?" he asked mockingly.

"You beast!" she raged. "You awful, stinking, dirty beast!"

Spain chuckled and held her tight while she sobbed hysterically. This was the most loco deal he'd ever been mixed up in. He thought, Kidnaping a whore! and was aware of the strong perfume she used. There was something about the exotic scent that stirred his imagination, that made him wonder how this blonde trollop would be if she really liked a man. It was an odd thing about women. Their appeal didn't involve respect, or even admiration. Mostly it was simply that they were female, the eternal magnet that pulled at every man's secret yearning for love. That, he supposed, explained why Joe Pratt worshiped this voluptuous teaser.

"Are you Clay Spain?" Lilybelle asked at last.

"Yes."

She thought about that for a moment

before asking, "Why didn't you say so?"

"What difference would that have made?"

She didn't say anything, but she was no longer rigidly braced against his arm. She lay relaxed, her head cradled on his shoulder, her disordered hair brushing his cheek.

Cap said, "There's Purdy's lights. We made a fast trip."

"For which I'm much obliged," Spain said. "I couldn't have done this for Joe without your help, Cap."

"Glad to do a favor," the liveryman said.

As Cap turned the team into the yard, Spain said to Lilybelle, "You be nice to Joe, hear?"

"You can't make me be nice to him," she said calmly.

"I can make you wish you had been. And by God, I will."

She snuggled closer against him, so that her body was a warm pressure. She murmured, "You can't make me — unless I want to."

"Then you'd better want to," Spain warned.

The rig had stopped now, and he got out.

Lilybelle peered out at the snow. She said, "I can't walk in that with these slippers."

"All right," Spain said, and took her in his arms. As he carried her toward the stoop,

Gail opened the door and called, "You'd better hurry. Joe is worse!"

Lilybelle ignored Gail. She whispered, "I'll be nice to Joe if you'll kiss me real sweet."

Not waiting for his answer, she planted her lips against his and closed her eyes. She was still kissing him when Spain put her down on the stoop. . . .

It was good to see Joe smile, to hear him say happily, "Lilybelle! You came!"

Joe would have this much to take with him: the conviction that the woman he loved loved him. It was more than most men had.

Women, Spain thought, were completely unpredictable, variable as a desert wind. He wondered about Lilybelle, who had kissed him so passionately before going in to hold a dying man's hand. Was it because she had to prime herself for an act of womanly compassion? Did she have to rouse some sensual warmth before playing her part with Joe? Her behavior didn't make sense, nor did Gail Purdy's. For Gail resented the kiss she had witnessed and seemed to blame him for it. She had scarcely spoken while he ate the meal she served him and Cap Ledbetter. She stood at the sink now, washing dishes while Lew Wade dried them.

"You want me to wait around and tote Lilybelle back to town?" Cap asked.

Spain nodded. "And Joe's body. Tell the undertaker to give him the best. I'll pay the bill."

"You going back to Cartridge Creek?"

"Right away. We're short-handed two men, and there may be trouble before morning."

Cap filled his brier pipe. He said, "That was downright heathenish, what they did to Seth Arbuckle. Puts you in mind of the Apaches."

"I can scarcely believe Sid would countenance such a grisly thing," Lew Wade said, plainly baffled. "It's beyond my comprehension."

Spain laughed at him. "There's a lot of things you don't know about your foreman, Lew." Then, very sober about this, he added, "You'll be needing a new foreman any day now. Sid Vivian is just about through in this country."

"You mean you're going to run him out?" Wade asked.

Spain shook his head. "I mean I'm going to run him down."

While Wade absorbed that grim announcement, Spain shrugged into his fleece-lined riding coat. He stepped over to the bedroom doorway and saw Lilybelle sitting beside Joe's bed, holding his hand. Moving close,

Spain could detect no breathing, but Lilybelle whispered, "Not yet."

"You'll stay with him?" Spain asked quietly.

"Do I have a choice?"

"No."

Lilybelle smiled and puckered her lips, inviting a kiss.

"Later on," Spain said.

"Promise?"

He nodded, and tiptoed out of the room. To Gail he said, "I'm much obliged for what you've done."

"It was for Joe," she said, not smiling. "You don't need to thank me."

Spain eyed her narrowly. He said, "You act like you're sore about something."

"Sore at you? Why, that's ridiculous. What reason would I have to be sore at you?"

Spain shrugged and went out to the barn. He was tightening the saddle cinch when Gail called, "Here's something for Sam," and hurried to him with a small jar of salve. "Tell Sam to rub this on his chest in case he catches cold."

The contact with her fingers as he took the jar did something to Spain; something past his understanding. It prompted him to take her into his arms, to kiss her protesting lips hard and hungrily.

Gail struggled fiercely. She pulled free of his arms, panting and excited. "You — you stud horse!" she cried. Backing through the barn doorway, she said derisively, "Lace Fayette, Lilybelle, and me — all the same evening. I hate you!"

Watching her cross the yard, Spain felt tempted to call her back, to describe the difficult time he'd had bringing Lilybelle here. But how could he convince her that the kiss she had witnessed was Lilybelle's idea, not his? And if he told her he hadn't called on Lace while he was in town, she'd think he was lying.

Then he thought, What the hell difference does it make?

As he climbed into the saddle and rode across the snow-carpeted yard, it occurred to him that only one thing was important: to find Sid Vivian and kill him.

CHAPTER TWENTY-FOUR

Spain was within three miles of Cartridge Creek when he heard the wagon. Its wheels, crunching over snow, set up a rhythmic disturbance in the frosty night. His first thought was that his companions had decided this was no fit weather for a roundup and had broken camp; that the snow and bitter cold had got too much for them. But almost at once it occurred to him that neither Earl Tipton nor Sam Purdy would quit in disgust. Hard on the heels of that realization he thought, Somebody got shot!

Dread stabbed through him. What if it were Pinky Troop, with his three small daughters? Or Pete Seely, or Bert Ingram? And suppose it was Sam Purdy? If Sam died, Gail would hate him for sure. It didn't occur to Spain that it might be Earl Tipton until he saw the wagon taking shape against the snow. Then it did, and he muttered, "Please God, not Earl." For Tipton's death, somehow, would be the worst of all.

Bert Ingram, alone on the spring seat with a blanket draped around his knees, was driving the team.

Spain asked, "What's wrong, Bert?" and identified Earl Tipton sitting in the wagon bed.

"We got raided this afternoon," Ingram announced, talking through a muffler wrapped around the lower part of his face.

"Pinky and I received wounds," Earl said, his precise voice tight with suppressed pain.

"Bad?"

"Neither wound is very serious," Earl said. "At least, I don't believe they are. Just painful. Pinky's hip is hurt, and my right shoulder."

Spain peered into the wagon, where Troop lay on his stomach. He asked, "How you feel, Pinky?"

"Felt worse and lived," Troop said. "What I need is a good drink of bourbon."

Spain turned to Ingram. "See that he gets it, Bert. Buy a bottle and charge it to me." Then he added, "Maybe I'd better ride along to town with you boys."

"No need to do that," Troop said. "We'll do all right."

And Earl Tipton suggested, "You'd better hurry on to camp, Clay. Sam and Pete are a trifle discouraged, I think."

"Suppose," Spain mused.

A trifle scared, too, he thought.

There was something here that needed saying; something important. For a moment, with a strong sense of depression weighing him down, Spain couldn't think what it was that he should say.

"Seems like luck is all agin us," Ingram muttered morosely. "This snow and all. I been wonderin' how the folks at home are doin'."

Spain knew then what it was he wanted to say, what he must say. Reaching out, he gripped Bert Ingram's shoulder in friendly fashion and said, "You go find out, Bert, soon as you get Earl and Pinky to town. This gather is busted."

"You mean you're quittin'?" Ingram demanded incredulously.

"I mean we can't whip Boxed W and the snow both."

Pinky Troop asked, "What about your cattle, Clay?"

"To hell with them."

"But it's not just the cattle," Earl Tipton insisted. "It's our crusade against Sid Vivian — and all he stands for."

Ignoring that, Spain said to Ingram, "Take these boys to town, Bert. Buy Pinky a bottle, and then high-tail for home."

"How about Pete and Sam?"

"I'll send them home too."

As he rode on past the wagon, Earl called, "How about you, Clay?"

"I've got no home," Spain said, and urged his horse to a trot.

It was an odd thing. Now that he had decided to go it alone, he felt better than he had for days. Not let down or disillusioned, but with a feeling of release, as if he had been freed of an intolerable burden. Wondering about it, Spain recalled the sense of responsibility he'd felt for his companions that first night in camp; the nagging apprehension that some of them would not return to their families. Even though Joe Pratt was probably dead by now, the family men would survive.

The sound of his horse crossing Cartridge Creek drew a challenge from Sam Purdy. "Is that you, Clay?"

Spain answered and saw Sam ride from behind a snow-draped thicket. Presently Pete Seely rounded in from west of camp. It was significant that neither man had been at the fire and that they seemed in no hurry to go to it now. Spain thought, More spooky than they've ever been. He asked, "What happened here after I left?"

"They spread out all around us," Seely said. "Five or six of them. They kept circling and taking pot shots at us."

Sam asked, "How's Joe Pratt?"

"Dying. Probably dead by now."

They thought about that for a moment before Pete asked, "You met the wagon?"

"Yes, and I told them this roundup was busted."

Sam eyed him wonderingly. He said, "Don't suppose we'd stand much chance, short-handed and all."

Spain dismounted at the fire and held his cold hands to the flames. "You boys might as well pack your bedrolls on a couple of horses and pull out."

"How about you?" Seely asked.

"I'll keep an eye on the chuck box and other stuff until Cap comes with a wagon tomorrow."

That seemed to surprise Sam. "You mean you told Cap to come for it even before you knew about Tipton and Pinky being hurt?"

"Yes," Spain lied. Impatient now to have them leave, he said, "Wish you'd get at it so I can go to bed."

"Won't take no urging to make me leave," Seely announced with frank eagerness. "By God, I'll be glad to git home!"

When they pulled out, leading two pack

horses, Sam said, "Stop by at the house tomorrow, Clay."

Spain nodded, but he thought, Not tomorrow. When he heard them cross the creek he turned to the chuck box and chose the food and utensils he would need. Then, using his knife on the tarp windbreak, he cut a yard-wide strip of canvas. A man couldn't use a pack horse on the kind of trip he was taking, but he had to eat and he had to sleep.

Sid Vivian was as miserable as a man could be. He sat close to the kitchen stove, holding the left side of his face to the hot oven, from which Charlie Ming had taken a pan of biscuits. Last night's long ride in the windy cold had stirred up an old and vicious enemy of Sid's: neuralgia. It inevitably settled in his left jaw and ear, so that he suffered the twin hells of toothache and earache, made worse now by the sniffles.

The five men, eating at the long kitchen table, ignored him. One of them had frostbitten ears; another claimed that both his big toes had been frozen. All of them needed sleep. When they had ridden in at noon, reporting no sign of Lew Wade, Sid had cursed them into renewed searching. But the crew had come back empty-handed.

Blacky Linkervale reported no sign of

Wade at Cartridge Creek. "We couldn't get very close with the snow on the ground," he explained. "They could see us coming. But we knocked two of them off their horses at long range."

Sid sneezed and uttered a croaking curse. "Charlie, rub some more arnica on my jaw," he commanded.

As the cook obeyed, Bill Umber muttered, "So that's what makes the biscuits taste odd — arnica."

"That stuff puts me in mind of a Ute squaw I camped with one spring," a line-camp rider said sourly. "Hadn't took a bath since August. She was what you call pungent."

"Stop your goddamn complaining!" Sid Vivian shouted. "You bums got it real good, if you only knowed it. Three square meals a day and a warm bunkhouse to sleep in."

The five men at the table considered that in silence until Linkervale said, "Red ain't got it so good. He's froze stiff, Sid."

"He ain't feeling no pain," Vivian said. "He ain't suffering like I am, by God."

"But he should be took to town and given a decent burial," one of the line-camp men insisted.

"We got no time to fuss with a dead man," Vivian argued. "We got to look for a live one. For our boss. Finding Lew is the important thing." He pushed Charlie away, snarling, "You'll take the hide off me, damn it." Then he said impatiently, "Don't you fools understand that if Lew should freeze to death or get shot, we'll all be out of jobs?"

"Might be a good thing," Bill Umber said. He got up and went toward the door. "I've had enough of this tough-luck outfit. I ain't hankering to end up a frozen carcass like poor Red."

Vivian ignored that, but when Linkervale got up, Sid said, "You've got to find Lew, Blacky. And he'd better be alive. Otherwise you'll be out of a good job."

"Good job?" Blacky scoffed. "What's so good about being choused out into the snow day and night? What's good about being shot at every time you turn around? There's a hoodoo on this outfit. Look what happened to Lin and Bob and Red. They was all rough boys that knowed how to handle theirself, and so was Kid Murdock." He shook his head and said flatly, "I've saw enough, Sid. More'n aplenty."

"You don't mean you'd quit?" Vivian demanded.

Linkervale nodded.

Sid stared at him in squint-eyed disbelief. "You can't do that!" he shouted. "What kind of a lily-livered bastard are you, any-way?"

That angered Blacky Linkervale. It stained his high cheeks and turned his voice sharp as he said, "I ain't lily-livered and I ain't a bastard. You think different, grab your gun."

Vivian remained bent over with his face to the oven. As if inquiring about a trivial thing, he asked, "How about the rest of you?"

A gray-haired line-camp rider said quietly, "I didn't sign on at fightin' wages and I don't want none. I'm leavin'."

Another, younger man said, "That Clay Spain won't quit. He'll keep naggin' at us till he chops us all down, one at a time. And so will them others. You ain't the big man in this country no more, Sid. Spain is."

The final speaker, a nineteen-year-old Texan, said, "I'm comin' down with a case of the grippe." He coughed. "I'm leavin' for town soon as I get my wages."

Vivian cursed in the low, throaty way of a man disgusted beyond anger or resentment. He said derisively, "I'll pay off when it suits my purpose."

"No," Linkervale said, and drew his gun. "You'll pay right now, Sid. We've earned our wages and you'll pay 'em, here and now!"

Vivian turned to peer at the gun. "Mutiny," he muttered, as if talking to himself. "Plain, outright mutiny." Then he said to Charlie, "Go get the pad of time slips on Lew's desk."

Afterward, when he was alone with the Chinese cook, Vivian said morosely, "What'd I ever do to get such misery?"

"You stay out in cold wind too much," Charlie said.

Vivian cursed. "I don't mean the neuralgia. I mean all this goddamn trouble. Lew gone. Maybe dead. Crew quit. What'd I ever do to deserve this? Always treated my men good. Never shorted them on vittles. Everything went like clockwork for years. Then all of a sudden the outfit goes to hell. By God, it's awful!" He sneezed, and held his face closer to the oven. "Clay Spain!" he raged. "That's what caused it — Clay Spain!" Sneezing again, Vivian yelled, "Put some wood on the fire, you goddamn heathen! I got to have heat! Heat, by God!"

By midnight the neuralgia was much diminished, thanks to Charlie's continued application of arnica and the heat of a roaring fire. But there was a new ache in Sid Vivian; a prodding, overwhelming ache that caused him to announce, "I'll hunt Spain and I'll kill him! No matter how long it takes, I'll kill him!"

CHAPTER TWENTY-FIVE

Spain camped in Big Arroyo that night, using a protected ledge against its west wall for a bunk. He got his sleep in long naps, replenishing the fire each time the cold awakened him and then sleeping again. It was snowing when he ate a frugal breakfast at first daylight. Crouched close to a dying fire, he soaked up the last of its heat. Sid Vivian, he supposed, would have his crew in the saddle now. The trick was to keep out of their way for a few hours. Saddling his cold-humped bay gelding, Spain thought about Joe Pratt, and took some comfort in recalling the little man's pleasure at the sight of Lilybelle last night. Joe wouldn't be missing the cold this morning. Or ever again. . . .

A bitter wind had risen by the time Spain rimmed out of Big Arroyo. This was at the south saddle, through which he and Joe had brought the first bunch of repossessed cows. It seemed like a long time ago. Quartering toward Mesa Parada, Spain rode slowly through successive drifts, which were knee-deep to the bay. This, he thought morosely, was a hell of a day for a showdown with Sid Vivian. A hell of a day for anything, except sitting inside by a fire. He was probably the only man in Apache Basin who'd eaten breakfast outdoors this morning. Earl Tipton was probably having his in bed about now, served by his adoring wife. And Sam Purdy would be having his breakfast with Gail. Spain thought, I should be having mine with Lace Fayette.

At noon he watered his horse at West Tank, where cattle had pawed holes in the ice. Then, with the wind behind him, he rode toward Boxed W. It occurred to Spain that this snowstorm might necessitate an abrupt alteration in his plans. If the crew had failed to leave the ranch this morning, he would have no opportunity to establish himself for a showdown with Sid Vivian. Considering this possibility, Spain weighed it in relation to his knowledge of Vivian's deep-rooted characteristics. It wouldn't be in Sid's nature to let a snowstorm interfere with a chore that needed doing; a chore that by now must have rubbed raw his brute instinct for reprisal.

The storm, Spain decided, wouldn't keep

the crew home, and Sid would be with his riders. That was one thing you had to say for Vivian: He never asked a man to do anything he wouldn't do himself. Come rain, snow, or sleet, Sid rode with his crew.

Spain wondered if Lew Wade had returned home today, and supposed he had. But Lew's presence shouldn't make much difference. Urging the bay to a faster pace, Spain thought, I'll have the cook fix me up a bait of food the first thing. With the Winchester cradled in the crook of his left arm, he peered steadily through slanting snow. Visibility was so poor that he rode within fifty feet of the ranchyard before the buildings of Boxed W loomed before him.

Halting at once, Spain took his bearings and changed course so that he would come up behind the bunkhouse. This was the touchy part — not knowing for sure if the bunkhouse was occupied. Halting again, Spain focused his eyes on the stovepipe and observed no sign of smoke; then he rode up close to the building's snow-flecked rear wall, dismounted, and led his horse around the south end. There was a window here, so frosted that he couldn't see through it. But that fact told him what he wanted to know. The crew was gone!

Confident now, Spain led his horse around

front and glanced at the main house. It was midafternoon, but he detected lamplight in the kitchen window. Leading his horse into the wagon shed, he tied the bay in a sheltered corner, and loosened the cinch. Carrying his Winchester, he walked through ankle-deep snow to the feed room. There wouldn't be time for hay. He wanted the pony tied behind the house and ready to travel fast when this was over. But there should be ample time for the bay to gobble some oats.

Using a bucket he found in the feed room, Spain scooped up a ration of grain and started back across the yard. He was within ten paces of the wagon shed when Sid Vivian called, "Who's out there?"

Spain dropped the bucket. In the heartbeat of time it took him to turn and glimpse Vivian, he wondered why Sid wasn't with his crew. That was Spain's chief reaction as he observed Sid standing on the snow-pelted stoop with his face oddly framed by a strip of red flannel drawn over his bare head and tied under his chin; bafflement, and a swift-forming sense of exaltation in the knowledge that he wouldn't have to wait. The showdown was now.

Sid's voice was a shrill screech ripping across the yard: "Spain, you bastard!" and his pistol was like a pointing finger.

Spain felt the whiplash of Vivian's bullet slashing past his cheek as he took deliberate aim with the Winchester. The rifle's successive blasts were like continuing echoes of the pistol's report. Vivian fired one wild shot as he teetered backward. A bullet knocked him halfway around. He was turning and trying to lift the pistol when Spain called, "This is for Joe," and fired again.

Vivian fell back against the doorframe. Then he tipped over as if pushed hard from behind.

Spain glanced at the bunkhouse, half expecting to see the door open. No sign of life there. Why, he wondered, hadn't Sid ridden with his crew? Recalling the red flannel, he thought, Sid had a toothache.

Lew Wade opened the front door now and called, "Is that you, Clay?"

"Yes," Spain said. Picking up the bucket of oats, he went into the wagon shed.

Afterward, when Vivian's body had been toted into the feed room, Spain asked, "Want me to have Cap Ledbetter come for it?"

Wade nodded, seeming dazed by the knowledge that his foreman was dead. He revealed no sorrow, merely bafflement. "You warned me this would happen," he muttered. "But I can scarcely believe it. Sid seemed so sure of himself — so confident that you couldn't stand against him."

Realizing how thin his margin of survival had been, Spain said, "I damned near didn't." For the strategic core of his plan had failed completely; intending to use the element of surprise against Vivian, he himself had been thrown off balance by surprise. Sid had seen him first, and had got in the first shot. That bullet, barely missing, had made the difference.

"Now I'll have to hire a new foreman, along with a new crew," Wade said.

"New crew?"

Wade nodded. "They all quit last night. Sid was the only one left." Then he asked, "How about you, Clay? It would be a good job. You'd receive half the profit the ranch makes each year."

The irony of it brought a cynical smile to Spain's beard-bristled cheeks. "One way to get a ramrod job," he mused. "Kill the ramrod. No thanks, Lew."

Presently, as he tightened the bay's cinch, Spain said, "Sam Purdy hasn't got much of a place. Maybe he'd take the job."

"A splendid suggestion!" Wade exclaimed. "He's just the man!"

Pleased with the thought, Lew followed

Spain out of the wagon shed, saying, "Please ask Sam to come see me. Tell him I'll build a house for him and his sister to live in, if he wants."

Spain nodded and climbed into the saddle. He said, "I'll be back for my cows when the weather clears."

"Of course," Wade agreed. "And my crew will help you, if I have a crew."

He was standing there, bareheaded and uncertain, as Spain rode out of the yard.

The wind went down at dusk. By the time Spain glimpsed the lights of Purdy's place ahead of him, the snow had stopped falling and the sky was clear for the first time in days. He thought, Storm's over, and in this moment he understood that the long storm that had begun in Sonora was over also. Six men had seen the beginning of it; only one had seen the ending.

Spain considered stopping at Purdy's for a cup of coffee and to tell Sam about Lew Wade's offer. Sam would be glad to know there'd be no more fighting. So would Gail. But she wouldn't be glad to see him. Remembering how furious she'd been the last time he'd seen her, Spain rode on past the gate. He could tell Sam about the foreman job tomorrow. There was a prodding impatience in him now to see Lace Fayette, to tell her the fighting was finished. Spain grinned, thinking how it would be. A woman's warmth and fragrance could make a man forget the long cold riding, the misery camps and cheerless dawns. A woman like Lace could make him forget 'most anything.

Spain urged his tired pony to a faster trot. When he finally reached the cattle pens at Hondo's west end, he peered ahead and glimpsed lamplight in the windows above the bank. She's still up, he thought, and let anticipation have its way with him.

Main Street was deserted, and so was Shiloh Alley. Cap Ledbetter came out of his harness-room quarters as Spain dismounted in the livery's lantern-lit doorway. He exclaimed, "I been wondering when you'd show up!" Then he asked, "Did you run into Sid Vivian?"

Spain nodded.

"You shoot him?"

Spain nodded and put his cold hands to untying the latigo.

"Dead?" Cap asked.

"Yes," Spain said. "How about Joe Pratt?"

"I brung him back to town with Lilybelle," Cap said. "Funeral is tomorrow morning. Funny thing about Lilybelle. She cried like a baby when Joe died."

"Give this pony a double ration of oats," Spain ordered. "He's had a rough day."

Cap nodded. He said, "Those boys at Shirttail Flats will be happy to know Sid Vivian is gone. He caused 'em a lot of misery."

Walking past Fancy Anne's place and thinking about Joe Pratt, Spain felt a sobering regret. It seemed monstrous that the high point of a man's whole life should have occurred in this alley; that the pattern of his living had been so forlorn that the mock love of a blonde trollop could seem precious to him.

"A hell of a thing," Spain reflected.

But presently, going up the outside stairway at the bank, he recalled the last time he had held Lace Fayette in his arms, and he thought, This will be different.

Lace opened the door. "Clay!" she exclaimed, and stepped aside. "Come in out of the cold."

Her eyes were aglow; her lamplit cheeks dimpled with smiling. In this warm and cheerful room she was the living image of a man's campfire dreams.

Spain closed the door and dropped his hat on a chair. He gave the parlor a brief appraisal, saying, "Nice." Then he took her in his arms and said again, "Nice."

There was a moment while her lips and the perfume of her hair and the sense of her woman's body roused him. Then she put her hands on his chest, pushing him back.

"Don't be stingy," Spain coaxed, and tried to kiss her again.

"Please, Clay," she protested. When he released her, she said censuringly, "You need a shave and —"

"And a bath?"

She nodded.

A self-mocking smile slanted Spain's whisker-shagged cheeks. "The man has been dodging around in the brush for a week to do a chore that needed doing. When he gets it done and calls on his lady friend she tells him he needs a bath."

"But you do, Clay. And your whiskers scratch."

Spain laughed at her. "Fastidious Lace Fayette," he mused, and picked up his hat.

"Don't be angry, Clay. I'm so glad you came. Really I am. I'll fix you something to eat."

"Didn't come here to eat," Spain said.

"Then sit down and we'll talk."

Spain shook his head. "Didn't come here to talk."

He watched color stain her cheeks. He said, "I thought you really liked me."

319

"I do," Lace said. "I like you more than any man I've ever known. But I can't help being what you call fastidious. It's just part of me, Clay." She made an open-palmed gesture, saying, "That's why I keep this room neat and clean." She smiled now, her eyes frankly pleading. "Can't you understand, Clay?"

Spain nodded, and in this moment of depressing realization, he understood that it was more than wanting things neat and clean. She had a need for self-possession; an inherent self-sufficiency so strong that she couldn't respond to the passionate impulses she aroused. It was ironic that Lace Fayette, who stirred the maleness in all men, should be immune to a sensuality that clung to her like an intimate perfume. That knowledge spawned a cynical amusement in Spain as he turned to open the door.

Lace grasped his arm. "Don't be angry," she pleaded. "Don't think me rude."

"You, rude?" Spain asked, and loosed a derisive chuckle. "I'm the rude one, honey. I'm neither neat nor clean."

Lace came around in front of him. She reached up and grasped his shoulders and said, "I'm so sorry, Clay. Really I am. It was horrid of me to say that."

"No," Spain said. "It was honest. I like my women to be frank about things."

"Then I'm forgiven?"

Spain nodded. "Next time I'll be neat and clean when I come calling."

That didn't please her. Retaining the hold on his shoulders, she asked, "Will there be a next time?" and now, not waiting for his answer, she whispered, "Kiss me, Clay."

Lifting a hand to his cheek, Spain fingered the whisker stubble. He was like that, thinly smiling, when she pulled his face down and kissed him. . . .

Afterward, undressing in a hotel room, Spain thought about her farewell embrace and marveled at his reaction to it. She had seemed eager to please him, to share his need for her. But there had been no sharing, no response, merely passive acceptance. It was as if, possessing all else, she lacked the capacity for love.

"A natural-born old maid," Spain muttered. Thinking of the long miles he had ridden to find this out, he laughed at himself. A man lived and learned. But it was a damned shame that Lace Fayette wasn't what she seemed to be; that so much loveliness was wasted on a woman who had no real use for it.

CHAPTER TWENTY-SIX

Joe Pratt's funeral was held in warm sunlight at noon. Standing bareheaded beside the coffin, Spain remembered how Joe disliked cold weather. It seemed wrong, somehow, that the weather should turn warm and Joe not be here to enjoy it. There weren't many mourners, for few people in Hondo had known him. Sam and Gail Purdy attended with Lace Fayette, and Earl Tipton and his wife; Cap Ledbetter drove the hearse, and Lilybelle and Jack Benteen came.

When the simple service was over, Spain accepted Benteen's invitation to have a drink with him at the saloon. They were standing at the bar when Jack asked, "What will you do now, Clay?"

Spain shrugged. "I'd thought some of starting an outfit with my Roman Six cows. But I guess not. If Lew Wade will buy them, I'll drift." It occurred to him that he hadn't mentioned Wade's offer to Purdy. He said,

"I've got to see Sam before he pulls out."

But when he got to Main Street, the Purdys had already left town.

At loose ends now, Spain walked back along Shiloh Alley. Lilybelle and a dark-haired girl were sunning themselves on Fancy Anne's porch. Lilybelle called, "Hello, Clay," and smiled at him.

Spain said, "Hello," and kept going. He thought of having another drink with Jack Benteen, but he had no hankering for whisky or for Benteen's company. It occurred to him that there was nothing in this town he wanted. Not a damned thing, except money enough to pay Joe's funeral expenses. If Lew Wade would buy his share of the cows, he could ride out of Apache Basin tomorrow.

Spain went to the livery. Cinching up the bay, he thought, I'll stop in that dry wash and get my own saddle, and hoped the coyotes hadn't gnawed it. Joe's saddle was a trifle small for comfort on a long ride.

Out on the flats west of Hondo, he tried to cheer himself by thinking that he owned 250 cows. He said, "I'm not broke." But the sense of depression, of being wholly adrift and without purpose, remained. This, he supposed, was how it would be for him always: periods of high excitement, of risk and desperate struggle, followed by empty interludes of aimless drifting. Until a bullet fired by some other Sid Vivian didn't miss. . . .

When he rode into the Purdy yard, Gail came to the doorway. She didn't smile. She just stood there watching him come up and stop.

"I've got a message for Sam," Spain said.

"He's gone to Boxed W," Gail answered. "Lew Wade sent his cook for him. Said it was important."

"That's what I wanted to tell him."

"Then you know what it's about?"

Spain nodded.

"Well, must you keep it a secret?"

Resenting her attitude, Spain shook his head. Women, he thought, were the damnedest people. There was no understanding them. "Lew wants him to take the foreman's job."

Gail peered at him in disbelief. "Are you funning?" she demanded suspiciously.

"No. Lew has to have a foreman. He's going to offer Sam half the profits each year. That's the deal Sid Vivian had."

Gail thought about that for a moment. Then she asked, "Won't you have a cup of coffee?"

Spain shook his head. "Got to go see if I

can sell my cows to Lew."

"Then what?"

"Why, ride on, I reckon."

"Where to?"

Spain shrugged. "No special place."

"Just so you're riding," Gail said sharply. "Just so you're footloose and fancy-free."

"Well, what's wrong with that?" Spain demanded. "What's wrong with a man going where he likes, when he likes?"

"A man?" she asked. Color stained Gail's cheeks and some swift-rising emotion warmed her eyes. She was like a different person; like someone he had never seen before. In this moment she was a woman wholly aroused and wholly beautiful. Even her voice, usually so mild, held a throaty vibrance as she said scornfully, "You're not a man, Clay Spain — you're a saddle tramp!"

Spain grinned at her. "Last night you called me a stud horse," he reminded her.

But he was already turning back into the kitchen. And, to his astonishment, she was sobbing.

"I'll be damned," Spain muttered. He stepped down and went into the kitchen. "What's the matter, Gail? What are you crying about?"

She stood near the table with her back to

him. She said, "I'm not crying," and held her shoulders resolutely straight.

Spain reached out and turned her around. He looked into her tear-moistened eyes and saw more warmth in them than he had ever seen before in the eyes of a woman. He asked, humble as a man could be, "Do you care where I ride, Gail?"

She nodded, meeting his gaze directly. "Since the night I bandaged your ribs, Clay. Why do you suppose I changed my hair to a center part? I thought if you liked Lace Fayette's hair that way, you'd like mine. But you didn't even notice it."

A self-mocking smile quirked Spain's lips. Recalling a favorite expression his Uncle Bert had used, he said, "None so blind as those that will not see. But I see something now."

"What?"

"The most beautiful woman in the world," Spain said with the conviction of a man stirred by a tremendous discovery. "The woman I want to marry." Then he asked, "Will you marry me, Gail?"

"Yes, Clay. Oh, mercy, yes!"

And now, as she came into his arms, her eyes held all the passionate warmth and ageless wisdom of a woman wanting to share precious gifts with her mate.